Animal Attractions

Roxie looked at Miles and Sabrina through half-closed eyes. "I'm tired. I'll jussst go curl myssself up sssomewhere." She flicked her tongue at them.

Sabrina and Miles stared at Roxie in shock as she dropped to the floor and crawled toward Miles.

"Hello, Milesss," she hissed, wrapping herself around his legs.

"Back off!" Miles exclaimed, doing his best to push Roxie away.

"Hold ssstill."

For a moment, Miles and Roxie scrambled on the floor as he fought to pull out of her iron grip. "Man!" he exclaimed, finally shoving her away.

"It's been a strange day, Miles," Sabrina said with a sigh.

Sabrina, the Teenage Witch® books

Available from Simon & Schuster

Sabrina The Teenage Witch®

Hounded by Baskervilles

Mercer Warriner

Based upon the characters in Archie Comics

**And based upon the television series
Sabrina, The Teenage Witch
Created for television by Nell Scovell
Developed for television by Jonathan Schmock**

Simon Pulse
New York   London   Toronto   Sydney   Singapore

First Simon Pulse edition October 2002

Sabrina, the Teenage Witch ® & © Archie Comic Publications, Inc. © 2002 Viacom Productions Inc. Based upon characters in Archie Comics. All Rights Reserved.

SIMON PULSE
An imprint of Simon & Schuster
Children's Publishing Division
1230 Avenue of the Americas
New York, NY 10020

The text of this book was set in Times.

Printed in the United States of America
10 9 8 7 6 5 4 3 2 1

Library of Congress Control Number 2002100920

ISBN 0-7434-4241-5

To Rosy,
my four-legged muse

Sabrina

The Teenage Witch®

Hounded by Baskervilles

Chapter 1

Lately Sabrina had been swamped with work, both at her aunt's coffee shop and at college. Her workload had gotten so bad that last night she'd been too tired to finish *The Hound of the Baskervilles,* one of Sir Arthur Conan Doyle's most famous Sherlock Holmes mysteries. By the time she'd finished her other assignments, it was after midnight. She'd tried to keep her eyes open, but her eyelids had felt like lead. And there was no way she could do an energy boosting spell with her housemate Roxie studying at the desk right next to her.

So when Sabrina's digital clock had flashed one A.M., she decided to call it quits and set the alarm for seven A.M.—at least she could finish reading *The Hound of the Baskervilles* before her morning classes started.

But as Sabrina opened her eyes the following morning, she knew something was wrong. She felt too rested, and the sunlight streaming through her bedroom windows was way too bright for seven A.M. And to make matters worse, Roxie was nowhere to be seen—and her bed was made!

Sabrina glanced fearfully at her clock. "Eight-forty!" she gasped. She had twenty minutes to dress, eat breakfast, read the ending of *The Hound of the Baskervilles,* and get to biology.

Good thing I'm a witch, she thought as she pointed up a bowl of cereal and a cute outfit. *But that still doesn't solve the problem of how* The Hound of the Baskervilles *ends.*

Her professor, Dr. Kramer, called on her students randomly, and if a student couldn't answer her question, she was sure to embarrass them. Sabrina had even see this no-nonsense professor reduce tough football player types to Jell-O.

It'll be just my luck that she'll ask me something about the end of the book the one time I didn't finish it. She'll embarrass me so badly that I'll have to go to the Other Realm to get my ego massaged—Aunt Zelda says it works like a charm.

Sabrina thought fast. What better way to learn about a book than to consult its main character? And way more exciting than reading Cliff's Notes.

2

Concentrating hard, Sabrina pointed at the air and whispered,

"Sherlock Holmes,
Wherever he roams,
Please send him to me,
On the count of three:
One, two, three!"

Sabrina snapped her fingers. Without missing a beat, Sherlock Holmes arrived in her room in a swirl of misty sparkles.

"Woo-hoo!" Sabrina said, thrilled to be meeting one of her favorite fictional characters. "Sherlock! You look exactly like I imagined you, with your pipe and tweed cap."

"Young lady." He cocked his head. "Your distinct accent tells me you're an American from the state of Massachusetts."

"Sherlock, as usual your powers of deduction are right on," Sabrina answered. "But enough about me. I need to know what happened at the end of *The Hound of the Baskervilles*—and fast."

Sherlock puffed on his pipe for a moment, looking fondly into the distance. "Ah, yes. The hound of the Baskervilles! What an amazing and terrifying creature he was, and what an unusual family those Baskervilles were. That was one of my favorite cases, and I'd be happy to tell you about it. But why would a household servant like yourself want information on the Baskerville case?"

"Whoa now, Sherlock. Household servant?"

"You come from a long line of household servants. I deduce from the shape of your fingers that your family has been handling brooms for generations."

Sabrina grimaced. *He's good!* "Well, it's more like vacuum cleaners these days, Sherlock. But what about that ending? Remember? Big dog? Baskerville family? Pressed for time?" Sabrina didn't mean to be rude, but she only had fifteen minutes to get to class.

"Give me your name, young lady, and then I will reveal to you how that strange case ended," Sherlock said.

"My name is Sabrina Spellman. Now, please tell all."

"Elementary, my dear Sabrina," Sherlock said gallantly. But just as he opened his mouth to go on, there was a loud knock at the bedroom door.

"Sabrina! Is there a man in our room?" Roxie asked, her voice tinged with suspicion.

"No way!" Sabrina shot back.

"I heard a man's voice," Roxie insisted. "I mean, it's not really my business, except that I need to get my science book and we're both late for class."

"A man?" Morgan Cavanaugh, their R.A., echoed from outside the door. "Is he cute?"

Sabrina slapped her forehead in frustration. Now she'd never get to hear Sherlock's story.

Sabrina pushed Sherlock toward her closet before he could protest. "Get in there, Sherlock, and don't make a sound. Oh, and try not to stink up my clothes with your pipe." Sabrina shut the door just as Roxie and Morgan stepped into the room.

"Where's the guy?" Morgan asked hopefully, her blue eyes wide with curiosity. "And what's with the smell?"

"What are you talking about?" Sabrina asked, smoothing down her long blond hair. "I had the radio on, that's all, and uh . . . I was trying out some new incense."

Disappointment swept over Morgan's pretty face. "Too bad. I was looking forward to meeting someone exciting. But seriously, Sabrina," Morgan went on, "we're all late for Animal Communications, and I need advice. Which boots should I wear? The red ones or the purple ones? I don't want to make a mistake with the color, or Dr. Cartwright might lower my grade." She pointed her boots at Sabrina, a different color on each foot.

"Dr. Cartwright's not going to notice your boots, Morgan," Roxie said, rummaging through her desk drawer. "But he will notice if we're all late."

"Speaking of late, Roxie, did you turn off our alarm this morning?" Sabrina asked.

Roxie stopped in her tracks, looking chagrined. "Yeah. After it buzzed for, like, two minutes. I tried to wake you, but you just wouldn't budge. Glad to see you're among the living."

"Barely," Sabrina said. "You guys better go ahead. I need a few more minutes here."

"All right." Roxie scooted out the door, practically closing it on Morgan's boot tips as she followed her.

"Color, Roxie, color?" Morgan's voice wafted through the closed door as Sabrina ran to her closet to free Sherlock.

"You possess an odd wardrobe, young lady," Sherlock commented as he stepped out from between some of Sabrina's favorite miniskirts. "Very futuristic fabrics. Are you a dabbler in science fiction?"

Sabrina thought of her life as a witch and of her occasional travels to the Other Realm. Would that

qualify her under Sherlock's definition of a science fiction dabbler?

"Or maybe your clothes reflect an American
fashion trend that hasn't taken hold in London
yet," Sherlock continued. "In any case, you
couldn't wear those short skirts on the streets of
London."

"Sherlock," Sabrina cut in, "how about the
super-abridged version of the story? I'm already
late."

"It was one of my most challenging cases, and I
solved it expertly, with a bit of Dr. Watson's help
at the end."

"End? Good word. I like it," Sabrina said en-
couragingly. "Now, tell me about that end.
Please."

"Not so fast, Sabrina," Sherlock said, tapping
on his pipe. "I like to know why my clients want
certain information from me. Why are you so anxious to learn this case?"

"Let's just say I'm working on a case of my
own—the case of the student who's going to flunk
English."

"All right, then. I'll do my best to help you."

"Thanks, Sherlock," Sabrina said, slumping
down in her chair with relief.

While Sherlock explained the story of *The Hound*

of the Baskervilles, Sabrina perked up. *This guy is pretty cool!* He made the plot of the book come alive. She could almost feel as if she were picking her way through a treacherous marsh on a spooky moor in southern England with an enormous, vicious, red-eyed hound chasing her.

Sabrina listened, enthralled. But as Sherlock wrapped up the plot, she began to feel a tiny shred of doubt. Was it cheating for her to have performed this character-summoning spell?

No way! She hadn't conjured Sherlock for help with an exam or a paper—just to save face in class in case she was called on. Her grade wasn't at stake, only her ego.

The more Sabrina thought about what she'd done, the surer she became of herself.

Conjuring the main character in a book is actually a useful educational tool. I mean, what's the difference between getting the scoop from Sherlock himself and doing regular old research, except that this way is a lot more fun?

Two minutes later, Sherlock had finished retelling the story.

"Wow, Sherlock, thanks. You were great!" Sabrina exclaimed, shooting up from her chair. "Now I can face Dr. Kramer without risking a major anxiety attack."

Chapter 2

Sabrina pointed at Sherlock. "Sorry we don't have time for tea, but I gotta go." And in a shower of sparkles, Sherlock disappeared.

There was a loud rap on the door. "Sabrina," Roxie shouted, "move it."

Sabrina opened the door to find a frustrated Roxie and a satisfied Morgan.

"I thought I told you to go ahead," Sabrina said.

Roxie pointed to Morgan and rolled her eyes.

"I think I'm right to choose the purple boots, Sabrina," Morgan said airily, looking down at her bright purple footwear. "Don't you?"

"Only if you want to blind Dr. Cartwright," Sabrina teased, grabbing her jacket from the coatrack and heading out the front door.

"Luckily, Newman Hall is nearby," Roxie commented as they hurried toward the magnificent

9

brick ivy-colored building that housed the various science departments at Adams College.

Sabrina's, Roxie's, and Morgan's first class of the day was Animal Communications, one of the most popular courses on campus, and *the* most popular biology course. Their professor, Dr. Mortimer Cartwright, was an award-winning biologist noted for his research on animal behavior.

But Dr. Cartwright was not only brilliant. He was also an extremely handsome bachelor with a shy but charming personality, traits that Sabrina's aunt Zelda hadn't missed for a moment. Ever since he'd started teaching at Adams this fall, Zelda had been totally taken with him. But despite an all-out campaign to attract him, he barely remembered her name.

"I want to get a seat in the front row," Morgan said eagerly, "to make a good impression on Dr. Cartwright."

"You've got lots of competition for him," Sabrina warned. "My aunt Zelda, for starters. But she claims he hardly notices her," Sabrina explained as she led them into Newman Hall. "She says he's really shy, and when he does talk to her, it's usually about his dog."

"His dog?" Morgan said, with a puzzled expression.

At that moment, Aunt Zelda appeared in the corridor. Her shoulder-length blond hair framed her attractive face which was all smiles. "Sabrina!" she exclaimed. "How nice to see you." Zelda nodded at her niece's housemates. "Roxie, Morgan." Lightly touching Sabrina's arm, she continued in a confidential tone, "You'll never guess who I just ran into—your adorable Animal Communications professor, Dr. Mortimer Cartwright! What a wonderful man. He even remembered my name."

"He's . . . multitalented," Sabrina remarked.

"You girls don't know how lucky you are to be in his class," Zelda gushed, looking starry-eyed at them. "Is everyone going to his award banquet Saturday night?"

"He's getting an award?" Roxie asked.

"It's very exciting," Zelda went on. "He's being recognized for his groundbreaking research on how ants and beetles communicate."

"And we care about this because . . . ?" Sabrina asked.

Zelda shrugged. "I have no idea. But you can be sure Mortimer Cartwright's discoveries will be central to the future of mankind. Speaking of the banquet, I've been on the hunt for an evening gown to wear. I want one that will get Mortimer's attention without being over-the-top."

"Oh, let me help you. I'm an expert shopper!" Morgan cut in.

Glancing at Morgan's boots, Zelda said doubtfully, "That's very nice of you, Morgan, but you'd better run along. Aren't you girls late for class?"

When the they entered the classroom, Sabrina was surprised to see a room full of students with no teacher.

"There aren't three desks together," Roxie said. "We'll have to split up."

Sabrina and Roxie took two empty desks in the front row. Morgan sat behind them.

A hush fell over the back of the room, and Sabrina craned around to see why.

Dr. Cartwright was entering the classroom leading a bowlegged basset hound on a short red leash. The dog's smooth coat was a patchwork of large brown, black, and white spots. His saggy eyes gazed soulfully at the students, as if he knew important secrets about life.

The class erupted in "oohs" and "aahs" as the dog waddled dutifully up the aisle. His short legs barely kept up with his master's long strides.

"Ooh, how cute!" Morgan said.

Is Morgan reacting to Dr. Cartwright's wavy brown hair, warm brown eyes, and cheerful manner—or to his dog's?

The moment he arrived at the podium, Dr. Cartwright turned to his dog and said, "Baskers, sit!"

And Baskers sat. He gazed up rapturously at his master, his ears pricked forward while Dr. Cartwright fished a dog biscuit from his pocket and tossed it into the air.

"That dog worships Dr. Cartwright," Morgan whispered, tapping Sabrina's shoulder as Baskers deftly caught the biscuit in his jaws, "and I can see why. Cartwright looks like a Greek god."

"That dog doesn't care what Dr. Cartwright looks like," Sabrina said. "He's just in it for the treats."

Dr. Cartwright had Baskers demonstrate a few more commands, including "down," "stay," "shake," and "roll over," each time rewarding him with a biscuit.

Then, facing his class, he said, "You may wonder, ladies and gentlemen, why I brought my dog here. Well, this class spent its first four weeks studying how animals communicate with one another, from snails to gorillas. We've done some fascinating lab work, including studying the intricacies of worm-to-worm communication, and we've done some interesting fieldwork, like when we went to Cape Cod and listened to migrating geese squawking flight signals overhead. What we haven't done yet is talk about how animals and humans commmunicate with one another. And that is why I brought in Baskers. Any questions so far?"

Morgan's hand shot into the air. "Dr. Cartwright," she said, flashing him a brilliant smile, "how did your dog get his name?"

Dr. Cartwright frowned. "Class, when I asked if you have questions, I meant biology questions. But since you asked, Morgan, Baskers's real name is Baskerville. I was reading *The Hound of the Baskervilles* when I adopted him from the pound, so the name stuck. Any more questions?"

Is this Sherlock Holmes theme day or something? Sabrina wondered.

She felt another tap on her shoulder. Sabrina whipped around to see Morgan looking out the open window at the back of the room.

"Isn't that your cat?" Morgan asked, pointing to a black cat in the window.

Sabrina did a double take. Sure enough, Salem was lounging on the windowsill, licking his paws and looking smug. The soft Indian summer breeze ruffled his black fur as he peered at the class with bright yellow eyes.

"What's he doing here?" Sabrina murmured.

Salem had once been a warlock but was serving one hundred years as a cat for trying to take over the world. In sentencing him, the Witches' Council had stripped him of all his magic powers, but they hadn't taken away his gift of gab. Sometimes Sabrina thought she and her aunts were the ones being punished.

"Lucky Baskers hasn't spotted him," Morgan whispered.

Obviously Salem was up to no good. Sabrina remembered that when she'd mentioned her Animal Communications course to Salem, he'd been intrigued. "I've wondered how these dumb animals know what each other is saying," he'd said. "I may just have to drop by and check this guy out."

Sabrina suspected Salem hoped to learn something that would help him regain his human form. Even though he talked—often incessantly—he still wasn't very good at communicating.

"If you don't have any more questions, class," Dr. Cartwright said, "let's move on. I want you to study Baskers when I give him this next command. Pay attention to the way he looks at me— look at his tail, his ears. Then tell me what you think he's trying to say."

As Dr. Cartwright ordered Baskers to sit, the dog gazed at him with his shy brown eyes. *Wow!*

It's true what they say about owners and their pets starting to look alike, Sabrina realized.

She felt her nose tickle, and as she sneezed a flurry of sparkles came out of her nose and mouth.

"Bless y—," Dr. Cartwright began, but then he stopped. Instead of finishing his sentence, he threw back his head, opened his mouth wide, and let out an earsplitting howl, exactly like a dog's.

The class sat stock-still. Not a paper rustled, not a breath could be heard. All eyes were fixed on the professor, including Baskers's.

The moment the howl died away, Dr. Cartwright began to sniff the air. He took one step forward and then another, sniffing, sniffing. "What's that I smell?" he asked in a strangely gruff voice. "I smell cat!"

Huh? Sabrina thought. *This guy's taking the demonstration a bit far.*

Dr. Cartwright's body tensed. Then he raised his hand and pointed above the room full of shocked faces.

Sabrina craned her neck to follow the line of his finger.

Salem! Dr. Cartwright is pointing right at him. Has he lost his mind?

"Cat!" Dr. Cartwright proclaimed. And he rushed down the aisle.

Salem leaped up, his back arched like a Halloween cat, his yellow eyes narrowed. The fur on his back bristled as he spat at his attacker. Whirling around, he leaped through the open window, disappearing from Sabrina's view.

Dr. Cartwright threw the window open as far as it could go, then scrambled onto the windowsill and swung himself outside.

"That Dr. Cartwright really goes the extra mile to teach his students!" a guy near the window said.

"I wonder why Dr. Cartwright hates cats so much?" Roxie said to Sabrina.

"Well, if he's not hanging around, neither am I." Morgan jumped to her feet. An excited smile lit up her face. as she shouted, "When the cat's away and the professor follows him . . ."

A wave of students stampeded toward the door, with Roxie and Morgan in the thick of it.

Alone in the classroom with Baskers, Sabrina shrugged. "The cat's away, but the dog's still here." Cocking her head at Baskers, she added, "What's with your weirdo master, boy? I thought you were the one who's supposed to hate cats."

Baskers leaped onto the desk chair near the blackboard, seized a piece of chalk in his jaws, and wrote on the blackboard: I LOVE CATS.

17

Chapter 3

Sabrina bolted upright in her chair, amazed by Baskers's message. "You can write?"

Can Baskers be a warlock in a dog suit?

Baskers continued writing. "Today's homework will be to observe an animal of your choice and report on its communication tactics."

Sabrina strode toward Baskers. Even though he was standing on Dr. Cartwright's chair, she towered over his squat body.

"So this is our homework?" she asked, pointing at his scribble. Baskers nodded, his droopy eyes staring solemnly at Sabrina.

"Since when does a basset hound give homework?" she asked.

But she had a terrible feeling about what was going on. First Dr. Cartwright was barking like a dog and chasing cats, and now Baskers was giving out homework. Sounded like some sort of switch has taken place. *Baskers and Dr. Cartwright must have switched bodies! But how?*

Sabrina glanced around the empty classroom, looking for a clue. Maybe there was a charm or something planted by another witch that had set off a spell.

Other than a canine prodigy, she saw nothing out of the ordinary.

She stared the hound full in the face. "Baskers, we've got a problem."

Baskers placed a paw in Sabrina's hand.

"I'm glad you agree, boy," she told him. *Uh oh—I just called Dr. Cartwright "boy."* "Dr. Cartwright, let's go find Baskers."

She snapped the leash on his collar and lifted the hound from the chair. "Your tummy is so soft and furry, Baskers," Sabrina said. "Whoops, I forgot again. Sorry. No more personal comments, I promise."

Okay, I know I didn't do anything remotely magical, she thought to herself. *So I won't get into trouble if I go to my aunts.* "Come on, Baskers," Sabrina said, tugging on the leash. "We're on a mission—to save a cat, a dog, and a . . . person?"

They hurried out of the classroom side by side. The main corridor of Newman Hall was deserted—classes were in session. But the moment Sabrina and Baskers stepped out of the building, she heard loud laughing and excited voices coming from a patch of lawn nearby.

Sabrina tugged Baskers away from the noise. She didn't want the other students from Animal Communications to see her sneaking off with Dr. Cartwright's dog.

A raspy voice wafted through the balmy fall breeze from somewhere on her right. "Come down here, you adorable ball of fuzz!" it barked.

Sabrina yanked Baskers in the direction of the voice. A couple of fierce growls led her down a path toward the edge of campus. There, Dr. Cartwright was scratching at the trunk of a large spreading maple tree, its leaves a brilliant Indian summer orange.

"Here, Kitty, Kitty, Kitty!" Dr. Cartwright called, his eyes fixed on the leaves above his head.

"Salem?" Sabrina called. "Are you in that tree?"

"In body, if not in spirit," Salem moaned from on high.

Standing next to the salivating Dr. Cartwright, Sabrina peered up through the branches of the tree. Hidden in a thicket of leaves, Salem glared down at her. "That man may look human, but his soul is pure hound," he said.

"Come on!" the professor called. "Don't you wanna play?"

Sabrina stared at Dr. Cartwright. "Salem, I'm sure he won't hurt you. He only wants to play."

"Never trust a dog, Sabrina," Salem said. "They're sneaky."

"I keep forgetting he's a dog."

Sabrina glanced at Baskers. He was staring up at Salem, his hackles as stiff as brush bristles. "A dog who's a man, who's wondering why there's a talking cat," Sabrina said.

"That should be the least of his worries," Salem answered, climbing up one more branch. The two-legged Dr. Cartwright began to scratch at the bark frantically. "We can play tag, and you can be *it*." he said eagerly.

"Just get him away," Salem begged, his voice breaking into a sob. "And lose the dog, too," he added with a nod to Baskers.

Sabrina sighed. It was hard enough handling a dog/man and a man/dog, but the cat wasn't making things any easier. "We'd better get to Aunt Hilda and Aunt Zelda's house. Maybe they can figure out what happened. What I do know is until Dr. Cartwright and Baskers switch back, we'll have to hide them from mortals."

"You mean barking up a tree isn't usual behavior for an Adams professor?" Salem quipped.

Sabrina gave him a look. Then she addressed the immediate problem. Turning to Dr. Cartwright, she said, "Forget about that stringy old cat, Baskers. I know a place where you can get some roast beef with a big bone on it, too."

Dr. Cartwright's eyes snapped with joy. "Take me there!" He sniffed the air. "I used to be able to smell roast beef a mile away. Wonder what's wrong. Oh well, lead on!"

Sabrina, Baskers, and Dr. Cartwright headed toward her aunts' house. Just before Sabrina turned a corner into the street, she stole a look behind her. Sure enough, a black furry form was scuttling down the tree trunk behind them.

A few minutes later Sabrina burst through the door of her aunts' big Victorian house not far from the college. "Aunt Hilda, Aunt Zelda!" she called. "I need your help."

Sabrina crossed her fingers that her aunts were home. It was mid-morning, and Aunt Hilda ran a coffee shop near Adams. But sometimes employees covered for her when she needed a break. Aunt Zelda was often home when she didn't have a class scheduled. Sabrina fervently hoped that now was one of those times.

Her hopes were rewarded. "What is it, Sabrina?" Aunt Zelda called, coming into the living room with Hilda. "Oh, hello Mortimer," she gushed, batting her eyelashes at Dr. Cartwright. "What a wonderful surprise seeing you here."

"Roast beef," Dr. Cartwright growled.

"Come again?" Hilda asked. Scowling at Baskers, she added, "Do you usually bring uninvited dogs into people's houses, Sabrina?"

"I'm glad you're both here," Sabrina said to her aunts breathlessly. "Aunt Hilda, this is my biology professor, Dr. Mortimer Cartwright, and his dog, Baskers. Only, I'm not sure right now which is which."

"What are you talking about, Sabrina?" Zelda asked. "And why aren't either one of you in class?"

Sabrina's stomach clenched. In all the craziness about Dr. Cartwright, she'd forgotten about her next class—English—and it started in ten minutes.

The two-legged Baskers poked Sabrina in the side. "Roast beef. You promised."

"Sorry, boy—I mean, Dr. Cartwright. Oh, this is so confusing!" Sabrina pointed at her aunts' coffee table, and instantly a chunk of rare roast beef on a big fat bone appeared on a beautifully decorated gold-leaf plate.

"Oh sure, he gets the *good* china," Salem whined, appearing at an open window.

"He's a brilliant scientist," Zelda said, admiring Dr. Cartwright as he started tearing the beef apart with his hands and teeth. "He deserves the best."

"Well, he's acting like a dog, if you ask me," Hilda remarked.

As if on cue, Dr. Cartwright stood up from his meal and licked his lips clean. Then he sidled over to Zelda and licked her on the cheek.

"Oh, Mortimer," Zelda said happily. "I didn't know you cared."

Sabrina looked around. "Now where would Baskers be happy and out of the way? Maybe in the kitchen, where he can smell food."

Salem gasped. "You're not putting that cat-hating thing in my kitchen!"

"Watch me." Sabrina led the way into the kitchen, where she pointed into the corner. A big dog crate flashed into view, complete with a fleece bedding and a rubber hamburger. "The burger's so you won't get bored," Sabrina explained to the human Baskers as she tossed the roast beef bone into the cage as a lure. He dove after it. "Good boy. Take a nap." She latched the door of the crate behind him.

"Sabrina! What are you doing?" Zelda exclaimed.

Sabrina held up her hands. "I can explain everything. Dr. Cartwright is Baskers, and Baskers is Dr. Cartwright. Just don't ask me why."

"Why not?" Hilda and Zelda asked simultaneously.

"Because I don't have a clue."

Zelda peered at both hound and human. "Looks like a switching spell to me," she concluded.

"Classic symptoms," Hilda said, watching Dr. Cartwright gnaw on his bone and Baskers study Zelda's class schedule on the refrigerator.

"And you have no idea how this could have happened?" Zelda sked her niece.

Sabrina raised her hands in a gesture of innocence. "I swear I didn't do anything . . . this time. So how do we reverse the spell?"

Distracted, Zelda looked curiously at the droopy eyed hound. "You're really Mortimer Cartwright?" She smiled. "I can believe it. You're a very handsome animal. Would you mind if I pet you?"

Dr. Cartwright stared at Zelda, then sat, lifting his paw for her to shake.

"What wonderful manners you've got, boy—I

mean, Mortimer," she declared. "How are we going to entertain you while we try to reverse this spell?"

Hilda stared at the two houseguests. "I'm curious. When did this switch happen, Sabrina?"

Sabrina told her aunts the whole story, with Salem filling in a few details about how scary Dr. Cartwright had been when he'd chased him up the tree.

"He's a dangerous man. Don't let him out of that crate," the cat added with a shudder.

"We'll have to keep him in it until we reverse the spell," Zelda said. "Basset hounds are roamers. We can't risk someone seeing Dr. Cartwright hunting cats and licking humans."

Sabrina checked her watch. "I've got to get to class. Sorry to dump Dr. Cartwright on you. Would you mind keeping Baskers, too?"

"Of course he can stay, Sabrina." Zelda bent down to pat Baskers's back. "You've been through so much, Mortimer. We'll make you very comfortable here."

Hilda sighed. "This is going to get ugly, I can feel it."

"Roast beef!" Dr. Cartwright said from his cage. "Hamburger tastes like rubber."

"Well, it *is* made of rubber," Zelda said, bending down to the crate. "You poor dear, you deserve better than that. Shall I broil you some filet mignon?"

"Zellie, my head is spinning watching you zigzag between man and beast," Hilda said. "Can't you make up your mind?"

"I feel drawn to both," Zelda said, wringing her hands. "One's got Mortimer's fantastic body, the other his brilliant mind. What am I to do?"

"Take them both for a walk," Hilda retorted.

"I'm really sorry, Aunt Hilda," Sabrina said. "I don't have a clue how this happened, but I gotta get to class."

"Whew!" Sabrina said as she raced over to Adams. *I hope they can find a way to reverse the switch.* The thought of Dr. Cartwright asking for raw roast beef during his award speech gave her the shivers. His brilliant career would be over!

But Sabrina didn't want to think of Dr. Cartwright now, not when she had English class to conquer. Pulling herself together, she forced her mind to review what Sherlock had told her that morning about *The Hound of the Baskervilles*.

The meeting with Sherlock seemed so long ago! Still, as she ran, she remembered more and more of Sherlock's words. He'd been exactly what the doctor ordered: live Cliff's Notes. Not only did she learn the plot of the book, she felt as if she'd been at the Baskerville mansion with Sherlock.

By the time she slid into her seat in English class, Sabrina felt confident she wouldn't make a fool of herself.

Dr. Kramer swept into the room. The students sat still, preparing to take notes.

Facing the class, Dr. Kramer peered over her wire-rimmed glasses like a hawk surveying its prey. "And now," she announced, "for a pop quiz on *The Hound of the Baskervilles*. I hope you kids have finished it. This may be an open-book quiz, but if you haven't done your reading, you're in big trouble."

Chapter 4

The class groaned.

"A pop quiz?" Miles Goodman said from the desk next to Sabrina's. "If I'd known about this, I would have paid more attention to the book."

Lucky I conjured Sherlock, Sabrina thought. *Still, my chat with him is no guarantee I'm going to ace the quiz.*

"Maybe you shouldn't have spent so much time last night reading your magazine about alien life-forms in Siberia," Sabrina whispered to Miles.

Miles shot her a suspicious glance. "Maybe, but I didn't see you burning the midnight oil reading *The Hound of the Baskervilles.*"

"Uh, I got up early and . . . crammed," Sabrina fudged.

"I don't suppose there will be any questions about extraterrestrials?" Miles lamented, staring

29

anxiously at the paper Dr. Kramer was placing on his desk.

"You'll do fine, Miles," Sabrina said. "I just know it."

Miles shot her a nervous smile. For a moment, Sabrina felt bad for him. Miles was the fourth housemate in her off-campus house. Nice but sometimes a bit strange, Miles loved way-out science trivia. Even though he was a good student, he sometimes neglected the rest of his studies when interesting stuff about UFOs came his way. And his new magazine, *Aliens in the Arctic,* was supposed to be a real page-turner.

Dr. Kramer finished handing out her sheets. At the front of the class, she said, "Quiet please, ladies and gentlemen," with an icy stare at Sabrina and Miles. "It's time to start your essays. I want all of them finished by the end of class. Use quotes and examples from the book. Begin!"

Sabrina bent her head and began to write. For about half an hour, all that could be heard in the classroom was the scratching of pencils on paper and Dr. Kramer's tread as she paced up and down the aisles.

"I always look out for cheaters," she'd warned her class on its first day.

Am I a cheater? Sabrina wondered as she wrote

her final sentence. *Miles didn't have access to Sherlock's great wisdom like I did.*

Sabrina quickly pushed that annoying thought away as she proofread her answers. *These answers are my interpretation of the facts, not Sherlock's. And I think they're pretty good. No way do I need to share any credit. I mean, how was chatting with him different from reading the book?*

Sabrina glanced around the room at her fellow students bent over pieces of writing paper. *Am I the first one finished? I guess Sherlock really did prepare me.*

Dr. Kramer checked her watch as Sabrina placed her test on her desk. "Done so soon?" the professor asked. "We've got ten minutes to go. But if you're sure, Sabrina, I'll grade your essay now."

Sabrina winced. "Thanks." She returned to her seat just as Miles stood up to hand in his paper.

The moment class ended, Dr. Kramer called Sabrina, Miles, and two other students whose tests she had graded to her desk. "Congratulations, Sabrina. You got an A plus! I was impressed by your command of the subtle themes in *The Hound of the Baskervilles.* Obviously you have a special feeling for that book."

"An A plus? Woo-hoo!" Sabrina exclaimed.

"And your test was also successful, Miles," Dr. Kramer went on, "though perhaps you didn't match Sabrina's complete grasp of the material. Still, great job!"

As Dr. Kramer moved on to the other students, Sabrina and Miles walked together into the hall.

"So how'd you do, Miles?" Sabrina asked, nudging his arm playfully.

"B plus," Miles answered. "Better than I'd feared, worse than I'd hoped. Don't get me wrong, Sabrina, I'm thrilled with my grade, but I wish I could do what you did."

"Uh, what'd I do?"

"Cram at the last minute and still ace the test."

"Yeah, but I wouldn't advise that. Too stressful." And it was! Calling on Sherlock at the last minute and getting him to spill the beans had required fast thinking and verbal finesse. No doubt about it—she deserved her A plus. *Thanks, Sherlock!*

"I'm hungry," Miles said. "Want to get a snack at your aunt's coffee shop?"

Sabrina stopped in her tracks as her mind clicked away. *Coffee shop . . . aunt . . . oh no, Aunt Hilda and Aunt Zelda stuck with Baskers and Dr. Cartwright!*

"You just reminded me of something I forgot at

my aunts' house. Sorry, Miles, no time to eat now. Gotta go."

"I'll come with you, Sabrina. Maybe we can bring our coffee over there."

"Bad idea," Sabrina said with a tight smile. *Does Miles still have his little crush on Aunt Zelda? Maybe that's why he's so eager to come along.* But crush or no crush, there was no way could she allow him to see an eminent science professor sitting in a dog crate. "Uh, Salem is sick. He's very contagious—don't want you to catch it. Bye."

Without giving Miles a chance to reply, Sabrina hurried away. She approached her aunts' house cautiously, scared of what she might find inside. Had they found a way to reverse the switching spell? She sure hoped so. Today was already Thursday, and Dr. Cartwright was expected to make an intelligent speech at his award ceremony on Saturday night. Would his reputation suffer if he couldn't?

But even before she opened the door, Sabrina knew instantly that her hopes were in vain. The sound of shattering china and loud thumps greeted her on the doorstep.

She yanked open the door. Total chaos! Salem was crouched on the back of the sofa, ready to spring on Baskers as he trotted to the door to greet Sabrina. A porcelain vase lay in shards on the floor. Sabrina's heart sank. Her aunts obviously hadn't found a way to reverse the spell.

"This creature has got to go!" Aunt Hilda proclaimed, entering the living room.

"Which creature?" Sabrina asked. Salem and Baskers had merged into a battling lump on the floor.

Hilda crossed her arms. "The furry one, whatever his name is. Salem is terrified of him."

"Oh yeah. Salem definitely looks scared," Sabrina noted as Salem launched another attack on Baskers.

After a furious scramble, Baskers finally kicked Salem off him. The pooch then scurried behind Sabrina to nurse a scratch in his side.

"Poor Dr. Cartwright," Sabrina said, bending down to pat him. "Salem, don't even *think* of doing that again."

"Wouldn't dream of it," the cat said, licking his paws triumphantly.

Patting Baskers, Sabrina covered up a sneeze, but not before she and Hilda noticed a shower of colored sparkles coming from her mouth.

"Uh, Sabrina, are you feeling okay?"

"Fine, except for the sparkles, I guess."

"If that happens again, or if you're not feeling well, tell me, okay?"

Before Sabrina could answer, Zelda entered the room from the kitchen. She froze at the sight of Baskers licking his scratch. "Salem," she said, "how can you be so mean? Hasn't this sweet hound has been through enough already?"

"Puhleese!" Salem spat.

"Mortimer," Zelda went on, "I was just in the kitchen serving your counterpart a homemade key lime pie, but he said he'd rather have roast beef. How about a piece of pie to make you feel better?"

Baskers immediately perked up and began to trot after Zelda into the kitchen.

"Not so fast," Hilda said, stepping in front of her sister's and Baskers's path. "Look at this place. Both of these animals can't stay here."

"Salem you go live with Sabrina for now," Zelda stated matter-of-factly.

"This is Salem's home," Hilda protested. "And look, Zelda. Baskers knocked over your favorite vase, the one that the Medicis gave you when you were a teenager."

But Zelda wasn't fooled for a moment. "Salem, you did that, didn't you? You and Hilda are in ca-hoots, blaming this terrible accident on an inno-cent dog."

"I resent the accusation, Madam," Salem said in his haughtiest tone.

"Innocent, sminnocent," Hilda said firmly. "He's got to go. I don't care if his inner soul is really a professor. He's got a dog's body, and Salem can't live with it."

"Why are you suddenly so concerned for the cat?" Sabrina asked.

"Oh, I know he's annoying," Hilda answered. "But I'm used to his brand of annoying."

"And I don't drool," Salem added.

"Well, there's only one other place Mortimer can go," Zelda said with a sigh.

Hilda, Salem, and Zelda all turned toward Sabrina.

"I can't have a dog in my house," Sabrina protested. "Roxie's even fiercer than Salem."

"But she's been declawed," Hilda countered.

"Plus, there's Morgan . . . and Miles. I'm sure Miles is allergic. He's allergic to air, for Pete's sake."

"Tell him to take a pill. I refuse to welcome this dog in my home," Salem said. He strutted into the kitchen, tail swishing.

Sabrina scrambled for help. "Aunt Zelda?"

"Well, as much as I love having Mortimer here"—she scratched the dog behind his ears—

"Salem *was* here first. It is his home. So I have to agree with Hilda and Salem. You'll have to take Mortimer, Sabrina."

Hilda waved. "Sorry, but buh-bye, Baskers."

Sabrina sighed. Clearly she was beaten. "Okay, you win. I'll find a way to keep Baskers in my house." With a sideways glance at Baskers, she said, "I know you'll be on your best behavior, Dr. Cartwright. You don't want my housemates to make you sleep in the yard."

Baskers lay down, placed his muzzle between his paws, and looked at Sabrina imploringly.

"Aww, he understands every word we've said with that dazzling brain of his," Zelda said. "Come on, Mortimer, let me cut you a big piece of pie for the road."

"Wait! What happened with the switching spell? Have you tried to switch them back yet?" Sabrina asked.

Aunt Hilda sighed, shaking her head glumly. "Never in all our six hundred plus years have we seen anything like this, Sabrina. Zelda and I checked everywhere. Zip. Nada. Nothing. Frankly, we're stumped."

"There's got to be something that explains it. And I hope we find it soon." Sabrina marched over to Baskers and gave him a hug. Once more, rainbow-colored sparkles poured from her mouth as she sneezed.

"There it goes again, Sabrina," Hilda said, frowning.

"Gesundheit," Zelda said.

"Have you been feeling poorly, dear?" Hilda asked. "You don't have a cold, do you?" She walked over to Sabrina and felt her forehead. "No fever, at least," she pronounced with a sigh of relief.

"I feel fine, really," Sabrina said. "I don't have a sore throat or a runny nose. Just a tickle sometimes that makes me sneeze."

"Sounds like a magical allergy," Zelda diagnosed.

"A magical allergy?" Sabrina said, worried. "Are they serious?"

Hilda shrugged. "Some are, some aren't. Some you can cure with a simple spell. But others, like Superabrecaditis . . ." She left off with a shudder.

"What's that?" Sabrina asked anxiously.

"It's when all your senses get scrambled," Hilda went on. "You start to hear out of your eyes, smell from your fingers—but I don't want to worry you, Sabrina."

"You already have, Aunt Hilda," Sabrina said. "Is Super whatever incurable?"

"Usually incurable, even with the most powerful potions," Hilda pronounced. "Plus, it becomes almost impossible to exist in the Mortal Realm without being found out as a witch—or, at least, as something really weird."

"You're scaring her, Hilda," Zelda said. "You know she doesn't have the symptoms of Superabrecaditis. At least, I don't think she does."

"You don't *think* I do?" Sabrina moaned. "That's not good enough."

"Now who's scaring Sabrina?" Hilda said. "Zelda, you know perfectly well the symptoms of Superabrecaditis involve sparkles flowing from the ears. Don't you remember having it when you were eighteen, and you couldn't go horseback riding with Henry the Eighth? You kept trying to put your nose up to his mouth so you could hear him. He was so unsettled, he nearly chopped off your head. Don't worry, Sabrina. You've got something completely different."

Zelda sighed. "The potion worked better in those days and I was finally cured, but not before Anne of Cleves caught Henry's eye."

"Why did the potion work better in those days?" Sabrina wondered.

"Unfortunately we witches have built up a resistance to it." Zelda's eyes fixed on Sabrina anxiously. "I'm sure you don't have Superabreca-ditis, Sabrina. Your sneezing is probably due to some allergy. In any case, I think a trip to the doctor in the Other Realm is in order. Just in case."

"A doctor?" Sabrina said. "But I feel fine."

"Magical allergies have a way of getting worse," Hilda said gravely.

"And mortals will begin to notice the sparkles if you're sneezing all the time," Zelda warned.

"Dr. Allerzapper is an excellent allergy specialist," Hilda went on. "He cured me of that wart allergy I had once, remember Zelda?"

"Ah, yes. You'd break out in hives whenever you came within ten feet of anyone who had a wart. And that was practically everyone in the Middle Ages." Turning to Sabrina, Zelda added, "You better get to the Other Realm immediately. I'll call ahead for an appointment for you with Dr. Finius Allerzapper. Whatever your problem is, dear, we've got to nip it in the bud."

"But what about Baskers?" Sabrina asked. "I thought Salem wanted him out of here."

"You think right," Salem said, returning to the living room. "And that creature in the crate is no joy, either. He keeps telling me he wants to *play*. My nerves are shot."

"Oh, Salem," Zelda said. "You can't have

everything your way. Mortimer is locked in the crate and can't get at you. And Baskers will go to Sabrina's house as soon as she gets back from the Other Realm. In the meantime, we'll shut Baskers in Sabrina's old room upstairs."

"Oh, the pain! The horror! *My* room?" Salem wailed.

"You can cope for another hour or so," Zelda said.

"Throw in a couple of tuna steaks and say no more," Salem bargained.

"Oh, all right," Zelda relented. She checked her watch. "It's time for me to get to class. Speaking of which, who will teach Mortimer's classes?"

"Zellie, you can't let a basset hound lecture a class, no matter how brilliant he is!" Hilda declared. "And the two-legged Baskers would just want to play Frisbee. I think Professor Cartwright is about to take a few days off."

"But his students are going to wonder why he's gone AWOL," Zelda protested.

"We'll get him to call in sick," Sabrina suggested. She zapped up a turkey dinner with all the fixings and told Mortimer what to say.

After punching in a number on her cordless phone, Zelda passed it through the crate to Dr. Cartwright.

"Mortimer Cartwright here," he said after a pause. "I'm feeling really sick. I'll be out for a day or two."

The witches waited during another brief pause. "It's heartworm, for sure," he added. "The vet says so." Zelda grabbed the phone before he could say anything else to alarm anyone.

Sabrina gave her "professor" his treat for a job well done. Dr. Cartwright gobbled away.

"Mortimer, you really aren't yourself," Zelda said, shaking her head sadly. "But we'll get you back on track for Saturday's gala dinner, I promise."

"One problem down," Hilda said briskly. "Now for the next. Sabrina, off to Dr. Allerzapper for you!"

Zelda sent a note through the toaster alerting the doctor to Sabrina's arrival. The teenage witch trooped upstairs to the linen closet, which doubled as a portal to travel to the Other Realm. "Good luck at the doctor's, Sabrina," Zelda called. "Mortimer will rest on your bed while you're gone."

"Give our regards to Finius," Hilda called out as Sabrina shut the door behind her.

A nanosecond later, she arrived in the Other Realm.

Sabrina walked up to the door of Dr. Allerzapper's office and went in.

A fat, brindle-colored bulldog sat at a desk. "Who are *you?*" the bulldog asked rudely.

"I'm Sabrina Spellman. Uh, who are you?"

"Wouldn't you like to know," the bulldog snapped.

An inner door clicked open. "Beatrice, who's there?" a man's voice called.

"A patient, Dr. Allerzapper," the bulldog replied, suddenly sweet. Hello, Ms. Spellman. My name is Beatrice, but friends call me Bea. I'm Dr. Allerzapper's receptionist. How can I help you?"

"I'd like to see Dr. Allerzapper, if he's not too busy," Sabrina replied, stepping over the thresshold into an empty waiting room. "I believe my aunt told him I was coming." The door behind Beatrice's desk was closed, with the doctor nowhere in sight.

Beatrice twisted her lips into a sly grin. "I'll check with the doctor. And mind you, don't go snooping through my things while I'm gone!"

43

Chapter 5

What's with the paranoid bulldog? Sabrina wondered, feeling totally creeped out by Beatrice. *Salem's attitude is a box of chocolates compared with hers.*

Sabrina took a seat in the waiting room while Beatrice checked with Dr. Allerzapper. After a minute, a bespectacled warlock with frizzy white hair poked his head out of the examining room door. "I'll see you now, Sabrina," he announced.

Sabrina stepped into the room, and Beatrice followed, waiting by the examining table as if she owned the place.

"Thank you, Beatrice, you may leave now," the doctor said firmly.

"Fine!" Bea growled. "Have it your way!" With an obnoxious leer at Sabrina, she waddled out the door, panting heavily.

44

"That's job commitment for you," Sabrina commented, once she and the doctor were alone.

"Low blood sugar," Dr. Allerzapper observed. "Bea's favorite kibble is on back order, and she's finicky about substitutes." He took out a stethoscope. "Now what seems to be the problem, Sabrina?" he asked, getting down to business.

"Well, I'm feeling okay, except that sparkles float out of my mouth whenever I sneeze," Sabrina explained. "My aunts think I've got a magical allergy, so they sent me to you."

The doctor took a good look at her and frowned. "When did you first notice the sparkles?" he asked.

"Just this morning," Sabrina explained, "when I sneezed in class."

Sabrina quickly told Dr. Allerzapper about Baskers and Dr. Cartwright switching bodies. "I think the switch happened after I sneezed," she finished, trying her best to remember the exact sequence. "Do you think it could be related to my allergy?"

"Slow down, Sabrina," Dr. Allerzapper commanded. "We haven't determined whether you even have an allergy."

Dr. Allerzapper took Sabrina's blood pressure and listened to her chest with his stethoscope.

Then, after examining her ears, nose, and throat, he said, "I have a few questions for you, Sabrina—all routine. First, does the full moon make your bones ache?"

"Isn't that a werewolf symptom?" Sabrina asked anxiously.

"Just answer the question, please."

"Bones ache? No," Sabrina answered.

"Does the sight of mistletoe make your heart beat faster?"

"No, but the sight of butterscotch ice cream does."

"Perfectly normal," the doctor said with a reassuring smile. "One more question, Sabrina: Do toads hop on your lap while you're sitting outside?"

"Haven't noticed any," Sabrina answered, grimacing.

"I'm going to take a few blood samples now," Dr. Allerzapper declared.

"Ouch!" Sabrina said even before the doctor took out a needle.

"Don't worry, I have a special no-pain potion," the doctor said. "It's a new development in witch science." Opening a green long-necked bottle, the doctor dabbed some of the steaming liquid onto Sabrina's forearm.

46

"My arm—I can't feel it!" Sabrina exclaimed a moment later. She turned away as Dr. Allerzapper gently stuck a needle into her vein and painlessly drew out some vials of blood. "Wow! No pain— no joke!" she said happily.

When Dr. Allerzapper had finished, he placed a Band-Aid over the needle prick and snapped his fingers. Feeling flowed back into Sabrina's arm with a pleasant burst of warmth. She stood up and faced the doctor. "So what's the diagnosis?"

"You definitely have an allergy, Sabrina," Dr. Allerzapper said gravely. "The blood tests should pinpoint what kind and whether it's the cause of the switching spell. Check with Beatrice in the morning for the test results."

"Not till then?" Sabrina asked, disappointed.

"Sorry. The labs are backed up. It's finger flu season."

Dr. Allerzapper opened the examining room door. "It was a pleasure to meet you Sabrina. Give your lovely aunts my best."

"Oh, I almost forgot. Back atcha from them, doctor. Thanks."

"Bea, I'll see my next patient now."

Sabrina exchanged places with a middle-aged witch who had a bright red rash on her face. "I get this whenever I eat apple strudel," she confided to

47

Sabrina. "But I can't resist—it's my passion."

"I'll be back tomorrow morning for my test results," Sabrina told Beatrice.

"As if I care," Beatrice replied, her lower teeth sticking out stubbornly. The evil look that Beatrice shot her made Sabrina shiver.

Sabrina stepped from the linen closet into her aunts' upstairs hall. She ran down the stairs in search of someone, but all she found was a note. Zelda had gone to class, and Hilda had to get to the coffee shop. Both Dr. Cartwright and Baskers were blissfully napping.

Sabrina grabbed Baskers's leash from the closet, then ran upstairs to fetch him. He was asleep on her bed, whimpering and pedaling his short little legs. "What are you dreaming about, Dr. Cartwright?" she asked, snapping on his leash. "Caviar?"

Dr. Cartwright woke up when Sabrina lifted him down from the bed. She thought he looked very put out. "Don't worry. I'm taking you to my house," she explained. "It's fun there. You even know some of my housema—at-choo!" The sparkles from her sneeze fizzed up into a plume above her face. "There it goes again. What gives? I've never been allergic to dogs. Beatrice didn't make me sneeze. So it couldn't be you, Baskers."

Baskers wagged his tail, knocking down a china horse on a nearby coffee table.

"Nothing to worry about," Sabrina said, "just a tiny token Napoléon gave Aunt Hilda. She'll hardly notice it's gone."

She dragged Baskers out the door. "Come on, Dr. Cartwright. I've missed all my afternoon classes because of you!"

Baskers cringed, glancing up at her with eyes she thought looked especially droopy, even for a basset hound. "I'm sorry," she said, melting under his sad gaze. "I didn't mean to blame this whole mess on you. I'm sure you want this resolved more than anyone."

Once home, Sabrina called out to her housemates, "Hey, I've got a surprise visitor here. You'll love him!"

The bedroom door flew open. "Who?" Roxie cried excitedly. "I was studying the Middle Ages, but I can always take a break." Roxie's eyes eagerly scanned the living room behind Sabrina's shoulders.

"Try foot level," Sabrina suggested.

Morgan hurried into the living room wearing a pink dress and bright orange boots. "Did you say 'visitor'? I'd love to meet him."

"There!" Roxie said, pointing at Baskers. "Sabrina, you snatched me away from medieval history just to introduce me to this . . . creature?"

"Does he shed?" Morgan asked suspiciously. "Because if he does, he's out of here. I am not spending half the day cleaning dog fur off of my clothes."

"Isn't that Dr. Cartwright's dog?" Roxie cut in, staring at Baskers curiously.

"Sort of," Sabrina muttered.

"Dr. Cartwright's dog?" Morgan echoed. "What's he doing here, Sabrina?"

She took a deep breath. *One tall tale coming up.* "Well, in case you guys didn't know, Dr. Cartwright is sick."

"He was acting pretty weird in class, remember?" Roxie said.

"Yeah," Morgan said, "but thanks to him, we had a great party."

"What's he got?" Roxie wondered.

"Some kind of flu, I think," Sabrina said quickly. "One of his, um, colleagues is taking care of him. Baskers was underfoot, so I offered—"

"No way," Roxie and Morgan said in unison.

"Dogs aren't allowed in college housing," Morgan added primly.

"Since when were you such a stickler for rules?" Sabrina asked. "Anyway, Baskers isn't any old dog. He belongs to a professor who needs emergency care."

"Doctor's note, please." Morgan asked, holding out her hand.

"I can get one," Sabrina said. If Morgan was serious, she could always use magic to conjure one up.

The front door swung open, and Miles appeared, shrugging off his backpack. "Hey, let's order pizza. I'm starved," he shouted. He stopped as his eyes trained on Baskers.

"Sabrina wants to adopt this animal," Morgan told him, "with no thought at all for whether he sheds."

"Hey, I just got all my prescriptions refilled, so I say let her keep him. He's cute, we could use another male around here, and he looks smart, too." Miles's face lit up as he approached the dog, who was sitting on his haunches and scrutinizing a remnant of newspaper on the floor. "Hey, can he read?"

Sabrina's horrified gaze flew to Baskers's reading material. The headline read: "Dr. Mortimer Cartwright to Be Honored at Saturday's Award Dinner."

"Don't be silly. Dogs can't read. He must see a . . . something crawling on it." Everyone jumped back at the suggestion. Sabrina pulled Baskers toward her room. "So that's settled. Miles agrees—we keep the dog."

"Hell-o!" Morgan chimed put in. "Can't you count? It's two against two."

Sabrina sighed. "But Morgan, I thought you wanted to impress Dr. Cartwright. What better way to a man's heart than through his dog?"

"Well, since you put it that way. Just keep him off my clothes!"

"And my bed," Roxie added.

Sabrina felt bad. Not only was she foisting an unwanted dog on her housemates, she was also exposing Dr. Cartwright to insults meant for his beloved dog. He must be so upset!

Maybe she could do something to help the situation.

"Hey, guys, I'll make dinner. How about spaghetti?"

"Yum," Morgan said. "And salad? Garlic bread? The works? A complete dinner is the least you could provide after dumping Cartwright's dog on us."

"I know, I know," Sabrina said. Now if only her housemates would leave her alone in the kitchen, she'd point, and presto—a delicious Italian dinner!

Maybe she could hurry them along.

She whispered,

"Housemates,
Out of my sight.
You've got homework,
To do tonight."

The instant Sabrina finished her spell, Miles, Morgan, and Roxie disappeared into their rooms.

Half an hour later, the four housemates were eating spaghetti and Caesar salad together at the table. While Sabrina had been using her magic to whip up dinner, she'd also summoned some kibble for Baskers.

"Baskers doesn't seem to want to eat," Miles commented. "Do you think he caught something from Dr. Cartwright?"

Sure enough, Baskers stood at the opposite end of the room from his kibble bowl. He gazed longingly at the spaghetti as the roommates wolfed it down.

Sabrina put down her fork. "Of course! That dog can't eat kibble." She shot up from the table, tossed Baskers's kibble, and replaced it with spaghetti.

"Waste leftover spaghetti on a dog?" Roxie cried. "Don't you know how rare it is for a college student to get a well-balanced meal?"

At that moment, the doorbell rang and Aunt Zelda breezed in, balancing several casserole dishes in her arms. "I brought oysters, filet mignon, arugula salad with goat cheese, and lemon mousse," she announced.

"Wonderful!" Morgan said. "And I've still got room for it all."

"But it's not for you, dear," Zelda said. "It's for the dog."

The mortals were speechless as Zelda prepared a platter of marvelous smelling food for Baskers and served it to him. "I do hope you'll like this," she said, doting on him shamelessly.

"Has your aunt lost her mind?" Roxie asked Sabrina.

"She acts as if that dog is hotter than Mel Gibson," Morgan said.

"Maybe the Arctic aliens have hit Boston," Miles wondered.

After Baskers gobbled the filet mignon and salad, Zelda scooped some mousse with a silver spoon and offered it to him. "You handsome boy, I brought your favorite dessert: lemon mousse."

"Mine too!" Roxie exclaimed.

"Professor Spellman, how could you?" Morgan said, watching in disgust as Baskers slurped the spoon clean with his long red tongue.

"Easily," Zelda said, happily letting the hound lick extra mousse from her fingers. "Good-bye, everybody. I've got to teach my night class on quantum physics." And with a hug for Baskers, she breezed back through the door.

Morgan plucked an oyster from under Dr. Cartwright's nose. "The dog won't miss it," she explained, popping it into her mouth.

"He was getting ready to eat it," Miles countered. "Sabrina, your aunt sure digs dogs."

Morgan brushed at her dress, causing a tiny puff of dog hair to waft into the air. "I told you. That dog is ruining my clothes!"

Why does Morgan have to be such a clotheshorse? Sabrina ruffled Baskers's fur. "I don't see much hair—at-choo!" Sneezing, she covered the sparkles with her hands. Morgan dropped the forkful of goat cheese she'd just sneaked and dashed toward the refrigerator. "Forget the rest of this junk. Must have carrots!"

Chapter 6

Morgan returned from the kitchen carrying a plate heaped with carrots, apples, and sugar cubes. Her housemates exchanged puzzled looks.

"What gives with the new diet, Morgan?" Miles asked. "Since when are vegetables and fruit high priorities for you?"

"She's always liked sugar," Sabrina pointed out, "but not like *that*."

Morgan ignored them as she crunched a sugar cube between her teeth. A car horn honked outside.

"What was that?" Morgan asked, her eyes wide with terror as she put her hand to her chest. Without waiting for a response, she bolted from the table, shying away from the front windows as she zigzagged around the room.

"Chill out, Morgan!" Roxie commanded. "It was just a car horn."

But Morgan barely heard her as she knocked into Baskers, who'd been trying his best to move out of her way.

"A-oooooh!" Baskers howled. He limped over to Sabrina and huddled next to her legs for protection, whining miserably.

"Poor Baskers," Sabrina said, eyeing the crazed Morgan in astonishment.

"A-oooooh!" Baskers howled again as Morgan raced upstairs.

"Pipe down, Baskers," Roxie commanded. "You're not the only one stressed right now. How am I going to study with Morgan clomping around above us?"

The galloping feet overhead shook the ceiling. "Don't be so rude to Dr. Car—I mean, Baskers. At least Morgan didn't trample you," Sabrina said.

"Well, if he were properly trained," Roxie replied coldly, "he would know when to get out of people's way."

Sabrina stooped to give Baskers a reassuring pat. *I wish Roxie's attitude weren't so sharp sometimes. She can be so venomous.* "At-choo!" Sabrina sneezed, carefully covering her mouth.

"Bless you," Miles said.

"I'm tired," Roxie said, looking at her house-mates through half-closed eyes. "I think I'll jussst go curl myssself up sssomewhere." She bared her teeth and flicked her tongue at them.

Sabrina and Miles stared at Roxie in shock as she dropped to the floor and crawled toward Miles.

"Hello, Milesss," she hissed, wrapping herself around his legs. .

"Back off!" Miles exclaimed, doing his best to push Roxie away.

"Hold ssstill."

For a moment, Miles and Roxie scrambled on the floor as he fought to pull out of her iron grip. "Man!" he exclaimed, finally shoving her away. "First Morgan starts acting weird, and now Roxie. What's going on?"

"It's been a strange day, Miles," Sabrina said with a sigh.

Miles brightened. "Hey, maybe it's an alien infestation. Have you seen any pods behind the house?" He jumped to his feet and peered out the kitchen window.

Miles turned from the window, his eyes shining. "Has this whole place gone nuts? Maybe Saturn's ring is responsible."

"Or Barnum and Bailey's?" Sabrina muttered.

"Lately, Saturn has been zapping Earth with powerful magnetic rays. Let me consult my astronomy book." Miles headed upstairs to his room. On the way, he added, "On the other hand, it could be sunspots. They emit laser beams. We're lucky we're still normal, Sabrina."

"Well, relatively," Sabrina said.

No sooner did Miles disappear than Sabrina turned her attention back to Baskers.

"Baskers," Sabrina said, jumping to her feet, "we are so out of here."

Sabrina snapped the leash on Baskers's collar, then opened the front door. *It must be that stupid switching spell! All I did was think of Morgan the clotheshorse and Roxie the vicious viper, and now they're acting like those things. I don't get it.*

I could really use some advice, and I can't ask Aunt Zelda because of her quantum physics class tonight. Sabrina headed for Aunt Hilda's coffee house.

"You can't bring a dog in here, Sabrina!" Hilda said sternly as they entered the coffee shop.

"You know he's not really a dog," Sabrina whispered.

"You know that, I know that, but what am I going to tell the health department?"

"Let me leash him outside," Sabrina said. "Then I really need to talk to you."

"Well, it's really busy. Maybe if you can help out for a little while we'll have time to talk."

Sabrina shrugged. A half hour more wouldn't make a difference to the current state of her housemates' behaviour.

Sabrina finished tying Baskers's leash to the leg of a bench outside. "Sorry, Dr. Cartwright, but this is just for show," she whispered before she went back inside to help her aunt.

After fifteen minutes of Sabrina filling customers' orders, things at the coffee shop began to slow down. She even had the welcome surprise of finding Josh at the end of the line. "Sabrina," Hilda called over to her, "things are just about under control. Why don't you chat with Josh for a bit and I'll come by in a few minutes."

"Thanks, Aunt Hilda." Sabrina got coffee for her and Josh, and they sat outside on a bench next to Baskers. Sipping his decaf, Josh said, "Sabrina, you won't believe what a great assignment Mike just gave me—taking pictures of one of the most popular professors at Adams, Mortimer Cartwright."

Sabrina gaped at him.

"I'd like to take them by tomorrow morning so

they can get in Saturday's paper," Josh added. "And I'm supposed to take more on Saturday night when Dr. Cartwright gets this big award. You've got a class with him, don't you?"

"Ye-ahh," Sabrina said awkwardly.

"What's wrong? Don't you like the class?"

"I love it," Sabrina said. "It's just that . . . Dr. Cartwright got sick today. I hope he'll be okay by Saturday."

Baskers barked from under the bench.

"Whoa!" Josh said, spilling a spoonful of coffee. "There's a dog under our bench."

"Oh, that's just Baskers—Dr. Cartwright's dog. I'm taking care of him until Dr. Cartwright gets well."

"He sure is a cutie," Josh said, his voice muffled as he leaned down to look underneath the bench. "How'd you get so lucky, Sabrina?"

Sabrina shrugged. "VIP connections."

Straightening, Josh said, "I'm sorry to hear Dr. Cartwright's sick. I wonder how I'm going to get pictures of him by my deadline."

Patting Baskers absently, Sabrina thought about Dr. Cartwright gnawing happily on bones at her aunts' house. *Josh will have to be as sneaky as a cat to get pictures of him without getting licked to death.*

"At-choo!" she sneezed, hastily covering a small tornado of glitter with her napkin. "Pardon me, Josh."

But Josh didn't say, "That's okay," or, "I hope you're not getting a cold, Sabrina." Instead, his response took her totally by surprise. "Coffee?" he exclaimed, rudely sniffing his cup. "How disgusting!"

He leaped up from the bench, then slipped inside to the sugar and cream bar. Seconds later, he returned with a cup brimming with half-and-half.

"Much tastier than a mouse," he said happily, dipping his head to his cup. Sabrina's cheeks turned red with embarrassment as Josh began to lap the half-and-half, clumsily splattering it around the table.

"This cream is heaven." A soft rumbling sound vibrated in his throat as he slurped the cream. Josh was purring!

"Is that dog still under the bench?" he asked, his face clouding over. He peeked under, then shrieked. "Help me!"

"Don't worry," Sabrina said. "That dog is totally tame. He even likes cats."

Josh was paralyzed with fear.

Hilda came out just as Josh was curling up in his chair.

"That's so cute how Josh is licking his hand and rubbing it all over his face!" Hilda said to Sabrina.

"Aunt Hilda this is *so* not cute. Josh just turned into a cat!"

"What? How?" Hilda asked as she took a step in Josh's direction, but the moment she got close to him, Josh jumped out of his chair and ran into a nearby grove of trees. "He's disappeared! We can't let him roam around acting like that," Hilda cautioned. "He could wind up in the pound."

"And he could have lots of company," Sabrina said. She quickly briefed Hilda on Roxie and Morgan.

"Did you sneeze when Josh became a cat, or when Roxie and Morgan became snake and horse?" Hilda asked.

"Yes, but Dr. Allerzapper's not sure my allergy is causing the switching. We should know when the test results are back tomorrow."

"Well, no matter what Finius tells you tomorrow, I'm convinced your allergy is causing it. It's too coincidental that whenever you sneeze, an unsuspecting mortal near you switches bodies with an animal."

"I guess I should stop making animal references." Sabrina admitted.

"If you ask me, you probably shouldn't spend any more time around mortals than is absolutely necessary until we find out what's causing this. You're a danger to them, Sabrina, not to mention to yourself. What if Miles makes you think of a grizzly bear for some reason?"

"I can't think of any reason Miles could give me to associate him with a grizzly bear," Sabrina answered. "But to be safe, I'll just hide in my room."

Hilda nodded. "And watch out for Roxie the snake."

Sabrina started to leave. "And it's probably best not to talk to Miles at all," Hilda called after her.

"Don't worry. He's too busy reading about sunspots to hang out with me."

Sabrina sighed. With Baskers beside her on the leash, she headed for home.

Streetlamps glowed like fireflies along the winding campus paths, lighting her way as she walked. Passing Newman Hall, she saw a familiar form approaching her from the steps.

"Sabrina, what are you doing out so late by yourself?" Zelda scolded.

"Don't worry, Aunt Zelda. I've got my guard dog to protect me."

"Mortimer? He wouldn't hurt a fly."

Sabrina brought her aunt up to date on Josh, Roxie, and Morgan.

Zelda's face turned grave. "First thing tomorrow, Sabrina, you *must* return to the Other Realm for your allergy test results."

Chapter 7

Back home, Sabrina fluffed her pillow and propped it behind her back as she sat up in bed. She was trying to study her Civil War history assignment and have as little contact with her housemates as possible, but the noises coming from the living room were distracting.

"What happened to all the granola?" Morgan asked in a high-pitched voice. "I've sworn off all food except grain."

"I thought you were on a carrots-and-sugar kick," Miles pointed out, his voice carrying loud and clear through Sabrina's closed door.

"They're good for a snack, but grain is what keeps me going. Oh, here's some oatmeal. I can eat that."

After a short pause came Miles's surprised voice. "You're eating it raw?"

"What other way is there?" Morgan asked. Sabrina heard crunching sounds.

Roxie's voice came next, but Sabrina barely understood her because she kept hissing her "s" sounds. "Did sssomeone clean up those dead fliesss by the windowsssill? I hope not, becaussse they looked pretty tasssty."

"Roxie, that is too gross. Are you trying to give me a heart attack?" Miles asked. "Sssorry. Don't mind me," Roxie replied.

"Don't *mind* you?" Miles exclaimed. "I mind both of you—*a lot*. I used to think it would be great to be visited by aliens, but I'm starting to change my mind."

"I think I'll go outssside," Roxie hissed. "I feel the urge to nibble on sssomething."

"Good idea!" Miles exclaimed. "How about you go to a late-night movie? And take Morgan."

"Great idea!" Morgan said. "Let's go see *Black Beauty*."

"Horses? Bor-ing!" Roxie replied. "How about *Raiders of the Lossst Ark*? The sssnake scene is awesssome."

"I don't know," Morgan said skeptically. "Sitting still for two hours isn't exactly a field of clover. I think I'll check out the track instead."

"The track?" Miles echoed.

"Then I'll go in sssearch of a man," Roxie said.

"A man?" Miles croaked.

"Yesss, a man who can play the flute or recorder and just . . . be totally charming. I could stare at a man like that for hours," Roxie said dreamily.

"Remind me never to take up the recorder," Miles said.

"I'm outta here," Morgan said excitedly.

"*Adios,* Morgan," Miles said, "and if you're heading for the track, bring plenty of cash and luck."

"Doesn't work that way, bud," Morgan retorted. "At the track, people bet on *me.*"

"Sssee ya," Roxie said to Miles. "Why don't you get yourself a flute sometime?" And Sabrina heard the front door close.

She turned to Baskers, curled into the crook of her legs. "This is giving me such a headache, Dr. Cartwright," she said, "but I promise we'll get you back into your regular body ASAP."

Baskers lifted his head and shot Sabrina a mournful look. Then he nestled into a comfortable spot at the foot of her bed. Minutes later, his gentle snores filled the air.

The night wore on, and Sabrina finished studying for history class. Then she began reading a short story by Edgar Allan Poe for her English class.

"Hey, Sabrina?" Miles said from outside her door.

Sabrina nearly jumped. She'd been completely absorbed in the frightening "The Tell-Tale Heart."

"Yes?" she answered.

"It's Miles. Can I come in?"

Reluctantly Sabrina said, "Sure." She didn't want any more switching accidents.

The door cracked open, and Miles's shaggy brown head poked through. His eyes fixed on Sabrina. "I just wanted to share this awesome news I read in *New England Dinosaurs*. It's one of the magazines I subscribe to."

"I figured," Sabrina said, trying to smile.

"They think that Champ—you know the monster that lives in the deeps of Lake Champlain?—might be the descendant of a type of dinosaur species that roamed the Vermont woods millions of years ago."

"Vermont didn't exist then," Sabrina said.

"Well, of course it wasn't called that . . . ," Miles went on, but Sabrina was barely listening.

Sabrina sighed, patting Baskers absently as he slept. *Why does Miles have to be such a drone? He always goes on and on about these kooky facts.* "At-choo!" she sneezed.

"ZZZZZ," Miles said.

"Huh?"

"Be right back." Miles's head disappeared from the doorway as he zipped into the living room. Seconds later he returned holding a large bowl and two spoons. "Want some?" he asked.

"Want what?"

"Honey. What else?" Miles looked surprised at her question. "Might I add that it's the very best honey I could find? Orange blossom." He licked his lips as he spooned some of the rich amber-colored honey from the bowl and held it out toward Sabrina.

Oh no! Is Miles a bee? "Miles, you're making a mess!" Sabrina cried. Honey dribbled from his spoon onto Sabrina's floor, forming a thick golden pool. "Thanks but no thanks. I'm not hungry for honey now."

"I was hoping you'd share it with me for dessert," Miles pressed. "I'll give you most of it. I always thought you were the queen bee."

"The queen bee? Great." Sabrina gritted her teeth and added calmly, "Thanks anyway for the offer, but I've got a lot of studying to do."

"Well, okay, Your Highness, if you're really sure. Meanwhile, I'll see if I can find some goldenrod to suck on." And he shut the door.

Your Highness? Aunt Hilda was right. I should stay away from all mortals until we figure out exactly what's going on.

Morning light poured through the waiting room windows as Sabrina entered Dr. Allerzapper's office to pick up her test results. Bea had been busily yapping on the phone and had barely looked up when Sabrina had opened the door and taken a seat. Sabrina was trying her best to be patient, absently scanning *Good Vibes,* a short newsletter featuring only good news, but Beatrice was being difficult.

Bea snarled as Sabrina finally approached her.

"I've been waiting here for twenty minutes," Sabrina said, summoning the nerve to interrupt Bea's call. "Are my test results ready?"

Beatrice sneered, holding her paw over the receiver. "Your results won't be ready until next week," she barked.

"Next week! Why didn't you tell me when I first came in?"

"Can't you see I'm on the phone?"

Sabrina took a deep breath. "But Dr. Allerzapper told me the results would be in today."

Beatrice shrugged. "What does he know?"

"A lot, I hope," Sabrina said. "Do you think I can see him for a minute?"

Beatrice shot Sabrina a withering look. With her lower teeth jutting over her top lip, she drooled shamelessly into the phone receiver. "You need an appointment," she informed Sabrina in an ice-cold tone.

Sabrina hesitated. "You know that I had one yesterday."

"That was then. This is now."

"But . . . but . . . Dr. Allerzapper told me to check back today for the lab results."

"Can't you understand plain English?" Beatrice asked snidely. "Your lab results will be ready next week. The lab technicians are out sick. Now, if you'll excuse me." She repositioned her slobbery lips over the phone.

"The technicians are *all* out sick?" Sabrina cried. "What's wrong with them?"

"Some Other Realm disease, I guess," Beatrice said vaguely.

Sabrina slumped back into her chair to collect her thoughts. She had to figure out how to switch back Dr. Cartwright and Baskers before the award ceremony tomorrow night. What if Dr. Cartwright escaped from his crate and made a speech to his colleagues about kibble?

Under Beatrice's beady-eyed gaze, Sabrina trudged out of Dr. Allerzapper's office feeling utterly defeated. Moments later she stepped out of her aunts' linen closet into their upstairs hall.

"Sabrina's been gone a while," she heard Aunt Zelda say from the living room. "I hope everything's okay."

"I'm beginning to worry," Hilda said.

"What if the test results are so devastating that she's paralyzed with horror in the Other Realm?" Zelda wondered.

"Maybe we should have gone with her," Hilda said nervously. "She's still so young—not even one hundred."

"A child, really," Zelda intoned.

"A kitten," Salem said fondly.

"I'm back, everybody," Sabrina said, descending the stairs.

"Sabrina!" her aunts cried in unison, rushing over to hug her.

"We were getting worried," Zelda said.

"Is everything okay?" Hilda asked.

"I'm sorry," Sabrina explained. "Dr. Allerzapper's receptionist kept me waiting ages only to tell me that my lab results aren't in."

"Come again?" Hilda said.

"Apparently all the lab technicians in the Other

Realm are out with some disease," Sabrina explained.

"*All* the techies are out?" Hilda repeated. "That seems awfully strange."

"The lab must have backups." Zelda said, her hands on her hips. "It's standard scientific procedure. I think I'll just pop over to the Other Realm and discuss this situation scientist to scientist with Finius. We can re-run the tests, and, between the two of us, I'm sure we can find a solution. You'd better come with me, Sabrina. Dr. Allerzapper might need another blood sample."

Salem leaped onto the sofa back. "Take me too!" he pleaded, rubbing his face against Zelda's arm. "That guy in the dog cage is starting to give me the creeps."

"But he can't get out. He can't hurt you," Sabrina said.

"I don't know," Salem answered. "I thought I saw him picking the lock with that wishbone from the turkey you zapped him."

"I don't trust you, Salem," Zelda said. "Are you up to something?"

"No," Salem said. "I'm tellin you I need a break. I can't even go into the kitchen without that canine Cuisinart threatening to cut me into feline fricassee. The taunting, the snarling—it's just too much."

"Poor Salem," Hilda said, scooping him up. "I guess you really have been suffering."

The cat gave a little sob.

"Of *course* you can go with Sabrina and Zelda," Hilda said, petting his soft black fur as he lounged on her shoulder. "There, there."

Zelda frowned. "Hilda, Sabrina and I are going to the Other Realm on serious business. Not as a holiday for Salem."

"But dontcha think I deserve a treat?" Salem asked innocently. "For being such a good host to Dr. Dog?"

Zelda rolled her eyes. "Okay, Salem, you win. If you're quiet while Sabrina and I talk to Finius, I'll take you to 1001 Flavors and get you a tuna-melt sundae."

"With whipped cream and a cherry?"

Zelda wrinkled her nose. "Yes. Just the way you like it."

Salem purred like a revved up motorcycle. "Thanks, Zellie," he said.

Moments later, the trio entered Dr. Allerzapper's waiting room and approached Beatrice's desk. The bulldog had her back to them and was yapping on the phone. *Has she even hung up the phone since I left?* Sabrina wondered.

Zelda rapped loudly on the counter to get the receptionist's attention. Beatrice swiveled her chair to face the new patients, her face like a thundercloud about to explode.

Suddenly her countenance changed. Her brown eyes were as soft as a spring morning. "Salem Saberhagen!" she cried. "Is it really you? I'd know that devious light in your eyes anywhere!"

"Bea!" Salem exclaimed, reeling backward. "You're a dog!" With his fur sticking straight up like a porcupine, Salem looked as if he'd just seen a ghost. "And quite the attractive dog, I must say," the cat vamped as he tried to recover.

"Gotta say the whiskers suit you, too, babe," Bea replied.

Sabrina grabbed the cat. "Excuse us a second, please." The Spellmans took Salem aside.

"Salem, how do you know Bea?" Sabrina asked.

Salem said in a tone of utter shock, "This *bulldog* was once the love of my life!"

Chapter 8

Sabrina gaped at Salem as he struggled to get a grip on himself. His ears pricked up, but his tail still looked like it had just had a perm. They returned to the receptionist desk.

Salem cleared his throat. "Bea, I'd heard rumors you'd been turned into a bulldog, but I refused to believe them."

"My story is full of sorrow," Bea whined.

"Seeing Bea must be a real shock for you, Salem," Zelda said.

"Of the highest electrical voltage," Salem replied. "You may not believe it, but this dog was once the loveliest angel alive. She could inspire the sky to rain diamonds."

"And flatten a few people in the process," Sabrina said under her breath.

"I see you are, ahem, displeased with the

Witches' Council as well," Bea observed.

"They can be so rigid," Salem stated. "And talk about unimaginative—you'd think they had enough domestic animals already."

"Well, better a cat or dog than a three-headed dragon," Bea said.

"Yeah. They are so not in these days." Salem laughed.

"And where would you find dragon chow?" Sabrina asked, trying to join in.

Salem and Bea gave her a look that let her know she wasn't really welcome.

"So, Bea, how did you go from hottie to hound?" Salem asked, cuddling closer to the bull-dog.

Bea quickly changed the subject. "What I want to know is, how can a cat be so darned hand-some?"

"Like anything, it takes work, babe." Salem threw back his shoulders and assumed a macho pose.

While Bea and Salem continued to get reac-quainted, Zelda took the opportunity to sneak by the desk and knock on Dr. Allerzapper's office door.

"Finius, it's me, Zelda Spellman," she called. "Can I have a word with you about my niece, Sabrina?"

Beatrice rapidly switched gears and swiveled toward Zelda, her face back in thundercloud mode. "How dare you disturb the doctor without my permission?"

Dr. Allerzapper opened his door and beamed at Zelda. "What a pleasure, Zelda," he said warmly. "I hope you're feeling okay."

"I couldn't be better," Zelda said. "It's my niece, Sabrina, I'm worried about. Her test results weren't in this morning."

"Who told you that?" Dr. Allerzapper said sharply, throwing Bea a look of profound suspicion.

Sabrina stepped up and briefed him on what Beatrice had said to her earlier than morning.

"I'm sorry to say my receptionist was mistaken," Dr. Allerzapper declared. "Your results came back first thing this morning, Sabrina, and the lab technicians were never sick." The doctor glared at Bea as she hopped down from her chair and lay on the floor in front of her boss. She put up her belly to be rubbed in a gesture of surrender.

"Get up, Bea," Dr. Allerzapper said. "That's not going to work.

"Break time is over," he commanded. "I'll have a word with you about this later." His eyebrows knitted together in a fierce white clump. "Sabrina and Zelda, come with me." He ushered them into the examining room and shut the door.

Sabrina felt a prickle of worry. Were her test results so alarming that the doctor had to talk to her in private?

"I'm sorry about my receptionist's behavior," he told the two witches. "She can be a real trouble-maker."

"I'm familiar with familiars," Zelda said, nodding. "But what about Sabrina? Is it a magical allergy, as I suspected?"

"I've got good and bad news," the doctor said crisply. "I'll start with the good news. I'm happy to say the test results are conclusive. They show that Sabrina has a guilt allergy."

"A guilt allergy?" Sabrina echoed.

"It's very rare," Dr. Allerzapper explained, "and it happens when a witch feels guilty about something. If she's exposed to an object that reminds her of her guilt, she'll sneeze. Have you done anything lately that's made you feel guilty, Sabrina?"

Sabrina thought for a moment. Other than foisting Baskers on unwilling housemates, she couldn't think of a thing. And the sneezing had begun before she'd brought Baskers home, anyway. "But I don't feel guilty," Sabrina said.

Dr. Allerzapper smiled at her in a fatherly way.

"Sometimes deep down we feel guilt without realizing it."

"But if I don't realize it, how am I supposed to figure out what's causing it?" Sabrina asked him.

"Let's try a different tack," the doctor suggested. "When you've sneezed lately, were you around anything different or special?"

"Just Baskers, my teacher's dog." Sabrina replied. "But I've never been allergic to dogs before and Beatrice didn't make me sneeze."

Zelda cut in. "Finius, what about the switching spell? Is it related to Sabrina's allergy?"

Sabrina briefed the doctor on the switches that had taken place since yesterday's visit and how she remembered thinking about animals in the case of her housemates' switching.

Once she'd finished, Dr. Allerzapper cleared his throat and said, "These guilt allergies sometimes have magical side effects."

He rubbed his chin as he pondered Sabrina's condition. "Sabrina, do you remember thinking about an animal in the case of your professor switching?"

Sabrina thought back to her class. "I do remember thinking that Dr. Cartwright looks a bit like his dog!"

Zelda noted, "Well, it's true Baskers is an unusually handsome canine."

"And the next thing you knew, Sabrina, Dr. Cartwright was barking?" Dr. Allerzapper asked.

"More like a crazed howl, but yes," Sabrina said.

Dr. Allerzapper considered Sabrina's story. "Here's what I believe is happening, Sabrina. We know your sneezes are triggered by some unknown guilt. Whenever you sneeze, there's a magical side effect that causes the human/animal switch. Your thoughts are linking mortals with animal personalities. In the case of Dr. Cartwright and Baskers, your thought that the man and the dog looked similar triggered the remarkable double switch. Fascinating, really."

"Excellent diagnosis, Finius," Zelda said. "What can you do to cure Sabrina?"

"Well, there's no cure per se. It would probably be best if you don't allow yourself to think of animals while you sneeze," Dr. Allerzapper counseled Sabrina.

"But what if I think of one by mistake? I can't always be thinking of not thinking. Isn't there something you can give me, Dr. Allerzapper? A potion, maybe?"

"What about a treatment at the Other Realm spa?" Zelda asked. "I had a delightful one a few centuries ago, and it did me a world of good. The mock-turtle oil they used in the steam bath cleared my sinuses. I didn't sneeze for another eighty years."

"Mock turtle is perfect for ordinary sneezes, but Sabrina's are different," Dr. Allerzapper said. "Guilt is an extremely sticky substance. Hard to get out of the system."

Dr. Allerzapper sighed. "Zelda, Sabrina, I've told you the good news. Now for the bad news."

"The good news wasn't very good. Maybe the bad news won't be so bad," Sabrina hoped aloud.

"As I said, there's no tried-and-true cure for a guilt allergy," the doctor began.

"So I'm stuck like this until guilt season is over? Why couldn't it be something easy like pollen?" Sabrina wondered.

Dr. Allerzapper peered at Sabrina over his horn-rimmed glasses. "It can be cured, but the cure isn't easy. There's no medicine that will make a guilt allergy go away."

"Nothing?" Sabrina gasped. "Not even pickled bat wings? I thought they were always the last resort for difficult diseases."

"Even pickled bat wings won't cure a guilt allergy," the doctor said solemnly.

"But we've got to switch Dr. Cartwright back before his party tomorrow," Sabrina insisted.

"Though he's made a delightful companion," Zelda remarked.

"Witch science has been working on a potion to cure guilt allergies for years," Dr. Allerzapper said. "There was a promising one developed from Dalmatian fur, but it hasn't been proven safe. A small number of the early case studies turned into fire hydrants. No one's quite sure why."

"Well, Finius, what do you suggest for Sabrina?" Zelda asked.

"The answer's very simple," the doctor replied. "Once Sabrina purges herself of her guilt, her allergy will vanish."

"And she'll stop turning people into animals?" Zelda asked.

"Precisely," Dr. Allerzapper declared.

"What about the people who have already switched?" Sabrina asked.

"Get rid of your guilt, young lady," Dr. Allerzapper began, "and the mortals you've switched will return to normal. They'll have no memory whatsoever of the switch."

"But how do I get rid of my guilt when I don't feel guilty?" Sabrina implored.

"The answer to that question lies deep within you, Sabrina. It's not in my power to help you find it," Dr. Allerzapper told her.

Sabrina thanked Dr. Allerzapper and opened the examining room door.

Zelda sighed. "Thank you so much, Finius," she said, "for getting to the bottom of Sabrina's illness. Let's get Salem and head home, Sabrina. Maybe you can work this guilt thing out once you're in familiar surroundings."

Sabrina stopped in her tracks as she and Zelda entered the waiting room. The musty air smelled overwhelmingly of fish.

"It's about time," Salem complained to the two witches. He was sitting with Bea on her desk. A huge cone topped with gray ice cream and herb-like sprinkles teetered in their clumsy four-pawed grasp. Together they lapped the ice cream, their whiskers tickling each other's cheeks.

"Bea and I ordered in," Salem explained. "I couldn't wait."

Sabrina sniffed. "Something sure smells fishy."

"Things *are* fishy, Sabrina," Beatrice said ominously, cuddling closer to Salem as she bit into the cone.

After another large lick Salem glanced up, his

lips slathered in gray cream. "Bea and I compromised on the flavor," he explained. "She wanted lamb. I wanted mouse. We agreed on tuna with catnip sprinkles."

"That's love for you," Bea barked.

Chapter 9

"The shock of seeing Bea has made me ill," Salem said, sniffing and coughing as he, Sabrina, and Zelda returned from the Other Realm.

"More likely the catnip sprinkles," Zelda said, feeling the feline's nose to make sure it was still cold and damp.

"I'll tell you one thing," Salem groused. "I'm writing a letter to that Witches' Council. How could they make a beautiful witch like Bea a bulldog? Why not a greyhound? Now there's a dog with *lines.*"

"I can't believe that Bea was ever beautiful," Sabrina said. "Her personality is so—"

"Lovely?" The cat struck a tragic pose with his paw as he perched on the telephone table. "Beatrice Bodenheimer-Brown used to be the most beautiful witch the Other Realm had ever known."

"Well, it's known at least one other," Zelda declared, primping in a nearby mirror.

"Did you and Aunt Hilda ever meet her?" Sabrina asked Zelda. "If she was that gorgeous, wouldn't she have been, like, Other Realm famous?"

"Bea was a legendary beauty," Zelda explained. "But our paths didn't cross. She had a wild reputation—and a wicked mean streak."

"Bea was so beautiful," Salem went on, "she could turn tiny kittens to stone."

"That's a good thing?" Sabrina asked.

"Medusa used to do that too," Zelda said. "But she wasn't exactly renowned for her beauty."

"Small creatures with weak nervous systems just couldn't take looking at Bea," Salem explained. "She was *that* striking. Anyway, we had a huge crush on each other. Of course, I was extremely handsome," he said, chuckling over his memories. "We made quite a pair. The stunning witch, the dashing warlock."

"So you still love her?" Sabrina asked.

Salem gave a little sob. "Would it horrify you if I said no? It's true, I'm shallow. Sure, she's still got a great spirit and a wicked sense of humor, but who could kiss that kisser? Maybe if she got that underbite corrected."

"You two looked pretty cozy sharing that cone."

"Hey, she was buying," Salem stated matter-of-factly. "And she said I could have all the sprinkles."

Zelda petted him. "Best to remember her the way she was then, Salem."

"On the bright side, her inner and outer selves finally match," Sabrina added.

"Speaking of her outer self, why was Bea turned into a bulldog?" Zelda asked.

"Why else?" Salem said. "As punishment for trying to take over the world."

"No wonder you two got along so well. Did she get a hundred years too?"

"It's the standard sentence," Zelda explained. "*Some* people get time taken off for good behavior, though."

Salem finished cleaning his whiskers with a flick. "I'm going to *ignore* that," he sniffed. "And I doubt Bea will wind up in the do-gooders club anytime soon. From what she was saying, I suspect Bea still has her old ambitions." A fond, faraway look came into his eyes as he added, "She was such a spirited woman—never the type to let anything stand in her way. Why should becoming a slobbering bulldog with no magical powers change her desire for world domination?"

"Why indeed?" Zelda said.

Sabrina shuddered. "That dog gave me the creeps from the moment I met her. I wouldn't be surprised if she's planning something as we speak."

"Bea is *always* up to something, and it's called No Good," Salem said.

"I wonder why she lied to us about the lab results not being ready." Sabrina said. "There must have been something in that report she didn't want us to see."

"But the report just said you had a guilt allergy," Zelda remarked.

"Maybe Bea thought it would somehow benefit her if I didn't learn the truth."

"Hmm. How would keeping your guilt allergy secret help her take over the world?"

Sabrina and Zelda were silent for a moment, thinking. "Hilda's more devious than either of us, Sabrina. Maybe she's got some ideas," Zelda said.

Zelda hurried down the stairs to see if Hilda was home yet. Sabrina relaxed for a moment on her old bed before Zelda returned. "Hilda must be at the coffee shop. Meanwhile Mortimer is sleeping like a puppy."

They talked as they walked into the hall. Salem had already settled into a favorite spot for a nap.

Sabrina was concerned. "How can we figure out what Bea's up to? I'm sure it's no coincidence that she withheld my test results."

The two witches turned in unison to Salem, who was nesting on top of a basket of clean sheets near the linen closet.

"I have the distinct feeling I'm being watched," he said, swishing his tail.

"You'll be our spy," Zelda told him.

"Do I get any spy gadgets?"

"Remember, Salem," Sabrina said, "the sooner we figure all this out, the sooner you'll have the house to yourself again."

"I would never betray Bea," Salem said proudly, lifting his head up high, "not for a million smackers."

"How about for a plate of fresh sardines?" Sabrina suggested.

"Deal," Salem said.

Seconds later Sabrina and Salem stepped out of the linen closet into the Other Realm. "Well, at least I'm not in the Mortal Realm zapping people into animals, but all this bouncing back and forth between realms is beginning to give me jet lag," Sabrina commented as she and the cat strolled into Dr. Allerzapper's office.

"Tell me about it," Salem commiserated. "I've missed two naps and my soaps."

"We're in luck, Salem," Sabrina said, pointing to an open window in Dr. Allerzapper's office building. "The window by Bea's desk is open. I can eavesdrop while you get her to fess up."

Salem drew himself up to his full height. "You don't trust me to deliver the truth?" he asked indignantly.

"No," Sabrina said without hesitation—or guilt.

Sabrina ushered Salem toward the open window. Peering through it, Sabrina saw that Bea was alone and that Dr. Allerzapper's examining room door was closed.

Rolls of furry fat cascaded off Bea's body as she squatted on her desk and studied a piece of paper with some writing on it. A manila folder lay open underneath it.

"Hee, hee, hee," she said, chuckling to herself, "that makes five mortals so far. Not bad for two days' work, Beatrice. Not bad at all."

"She's definitely up to something," Sabrina whispered.

"Not everyone who chuckles evilly is up to something," Salem said huffily. "Sometimes I do it just to keep in shape."

"Shh!" Sabrina cut in. "What does she mean, 'five mortals so far'?"

Bea gave a little yap of satisfaction before adding, "Five animal souls inside powerful human bodies. Mortimer, Morgan, Roxie, Miles, and Josh. And those are just the beginning," she crowed. "The world will soon be mine!"

"Okay," Salem said, heading for the portal back to the Spellman house. "Looks like my work here is done. I'm so good, I didn't even have to lift a paw."

"Not so fast, Sherlock," Sabrina caught the cat and held on to him. "We have to find out *how* she's doing this and stop her. Now comes the hard part." Sabrina pushed Salem toward the opening in the window.

"What I won't do for food. How humiliating," he whined as he slithered through the window.

Salem jumped from the windowsill to Bea's desk in a graceful, black arc. "Purr-fect landing!" he announced.

Bea gave a startled growl and skittered to the side of the desk as fast as her stumpy legs would take her. "What in the Other Realm is going on?" she barked. Then her eyes registered her visitor. "Salem! I knew you'd be back."

"In the fur."

Bea tried unsuccessfully to pull in her bottom teeth. Batting her wrinkled eyelids at him, she murmured, "Salem, my love, have you come in secret to ask for my paw in marriage?"

Salem arched his back in surprise, his fur standing on end.

Sabrina gulped. *Don't swat her, Salem.*

But Salem quickly regained control of himself before Bea noticed anything wrong. "There's nothing I'd love to do more," he lied. "But alas, we live in different worlds. It's cruel, but we're powerless to change it."

"'Tis true, 'tis true," Bea lamented. "But I could tell you were as smitten with me today as you were when we danced for the first time at the tsar's ball so long ago in Saint Petersburg."

"Yes, darling." Salem worked hard to keep up his ruse.

"Those were the days! We could plot and scheme and dance all we wanted, and nobody ever bothered us. We should have taken over the world then, while we had the chance."

"Yes, darling."

Bea's eyes narrowed, and her lips drew into a ghastly smirk. "Just because we failed to take over the world the first times we tried doesn't mean we can't try again." She sidled up to him. "We might succeed if we teamed up."

"That would be lovely, Bea, but I'm afraid it's hopeless. You're a dog, I'm a cat, and neither of us has magic—or thumbs."

"Who needs magic when you've got brains like ours? I've already got a plan in the works, and I'm days away from realizing it."

"Bea, you dirty dog," Salem said, impressed.

Bea grinned. "You'll love it. I just have to make sure Sabrina keeps sneezing from that guilt allergy. Once enough mortals have animal personalities, I'll rule the world!"

"How so, my darling?"

"Humans will be so easy to control. Animals will become their masters. And I will become the animals' supreme mistress. I don't need magic. Magic is just a crutch for mediocre minds."

"So if Sabrina keeps sneezing and switching more mortals—"

"I will triumph!" Bea finished gleefully. "Rule with me, Salem. We were magnificent together once, and we shall be again."

Salem was torn. World domination was tempting, but he couldn't implicate Sabrina in this crazy plan. Besides, he doubted it could actually work.

"But Sabrina knows the results of her test now, Bea," Salem pointed out.

"Thanks to that meddling aunt of hers," Bea said bitterly. "Still, Sabrina's only gotten past step one—Know Thy Disease. Step two is Cure It, and there's no easy cure for a guilt allergy."

The examining room door cracked open and Dr. Allerzapper poked his head into the waiting room. In a flash, Salem leaped back to the windowsill and slunk back through the opening.

"I could swear I saw a black blur streaking across your desk, Beatrice. I hope someone hasn't bewitched us," the doctor said, frowning.

"I'm under a spell, all right, Dr. Allerzapper," Bea murmured, gazing longingly toward the window. "A love spell."

"Get me out of here!" Salem begged, whispering into Sabrina's ear as they sneaked away from the office building. "I can't keep up the lovestruck act. I'm good, but I'm not that good."

"Aunt Zelda? Aunt Hilda? Are you here?" Sabrina called as she and Salem emerged from the linen closet.

"I'm in the kitchen, making Mortimer some lamb stew," Zelda shouted.

"Why are you yelling?" Hilda yelled back as

she came in the front door.

"We got the scoop on Bea," Sabrina said as she and Salem hurried downstairs. They joined Zelda and Hilda in the kitchen.

Salem rubbed against Sabrina's legs. "I did my bit. Now pay up."

Sabrina pointed up a plate of gigantic, super-smelly sardines. While Salem dug into them, she briefed her aunts on Bea.

Zelda shook her head glumly. "There's nothing Hilda or I can do to stop Bea. It's all up to you, Sabrina. You've got to figure out what you're feeling guilty about."

Hilda frowned at Salem as he licked his chops. "And the sooner the better, Sabrina." she said.

Chapter 10

☆

"I'm off to class," Sabrina announced. She and her aunts had just finished lunch, and Salem had devoured his sardines.

"You really shouldn't, Sabrina," Hilda said. "You're way too dangerous."

"Aunt Hilda, I already missed a class this morning because of my trip to the Other Realm. I can't fall behind because of some crazy spell I can't help."

"But you can help it," Hilda countered. "You can purge your guilt."

"Aunt Hilda, I'll never figure out what's causing my guilt if I stay cooped up in my room. If I just do the things I usually do, maybe I can figure out which one caused the guilt. So far the only thing I can come up with is that maybe I haven't been nice enough to people lately."

"I can't believe that's true," Zelda said kindly. "You've been very nice to us."

"Well, she's needed us, Zellie. Maybe she's right. Maybe she hasn't been as nice to her house-mates or customers at the coffee shop. Spill it, Sabrina. Whatcha been up to?"

Sabrina thought for a minute. "Okay, take Roxie. She can be really sarcastic sometimes. Maybe if I go out of my way to be nice to her, I'll get rid of my guilt."

"Roxie can try the patience of any witch," Zelda agreed. "Good thinking, Sabrina. You've got yourself quite a challenge. But you'll want to proceed carefully, remember she's presently a snake."

When Sabrina was halfway down the walk, Hilda opened the door and called, "Maybe you should take along some anti-venom."

"It's okay, Aunt Hilda. After living with Roxie for two years, I've got natural immunity."

After checking in at her house and finding no one there but the professor asleep on her bed, Sabrina collected her books and headed toward campus. It was two o'clock, which meant that her Civil War history class was just letting out. Thanks to her Friday schedule, Sabrina had an hour break until English began at three.

So where could she find Roxie?

Sabrina looked around to make sure she was alone. A line of bushes beside the path afforded her plenty of privacy. Ducking into the bushes, she recited,

> *"Roxie's schedule*
> *Please appear*
> *On this branch*
> *That is so near."*

Instantly a piece of paper materialized on a twig of the bush in front of her.

Sabrina pulled the paper off the bush and studied it. *Let's see. Roxie's schedule.* At two o'clock, Medieval History had just finished, and Twentieth-Century Music Composition was about to begin. *But will Roxie go to any of her classes in the state she's in?*

Still, music class was worth a try. Sabrina stuffed Roxie's schedule into her pocket and headed to Huppman Hall, the music building.

Once there, Sabrina consulted the schedule for the location of Roxie's class. But when Sabrina peeked into the large lecture hall, her heart sank. There was no sign of Roxie at all among the students.

Where would a snake be at two in the afternoon?

The sounds of various musical instruments floated into the hallway from the practice rooms in Huppman Hall. Sabrina recognized a piano, a violin, and a flute as she walked down the corridor.

A flute! Sabrina stopped, listening, as Roxie's last words before she'd left the house last night flooded back into her brain.

What was it Roxie had said? Something about going in search of a flute player. Maybe she had a snake charmer on the brain.

On a hunch, Sabrina followed the sounds of the flute as they trilled down the hall. *Bingo.* They came from a room at the very end of the hall.

Sabrina cracked open the door. To her delight, Roxie was lounging across some folding chairs as a tall, broad-shouldered, dark-haired guy practiced his flute in front of her. Roxie stared up at him, utterly transfixed.

Sabrina watched too. *I can see how she's charmed. This guy is a hottie.*

The flute player stopped playing as Sabrina slipped into the room. Catching her gaze, he made a crazy signal next to his head with his forefinger, then pointed at Roxie.

He thinks she's nuts!

"Uh, my friend *really* loves the flute," Sabrina said in a hushed voice. "But I'm sure you need to concentrate, so I'll just get her out of here. Just keep playing and don't mind us."

The flute player nodded, then got back to work.

"Hey, Roxie," Sabrina said, sitting down next to her. Roxie glared at her through half-closed eyes, then suddenly flicked her tongue. *Be nice,* she reminded herself.

"Hey, Roxie," she repeated. "Can I do anything for you? Maybe make you some tea, or find you a comfortable wicker basket to curl up in?"

Roxie sat up, still glaring at Sabrina. "I'm actually quite comfortable, Sabrina. What I would like is to be left alone with this *charming* man."

Well, if that's what she really wants, Sabrina thought. *I guess I should be nice and do as she asks. She's really harmless anyway.*

"Okay, but why don't you move over here?" Sabrina pointed to a corner out of the practicing flute player's line of sight. "It's nice and warm, and the music flows perfectly to this spot."

Roxie slithered to the sunny corner and curled up blissfully.

Sabrina headed out of the building convinced she had done the right thing and immediately recognized two figures on the gravel path in front of the building. Her stomach clenched. It was Morgan walking Baskers on a leash.

Morgan tossed her wild mane of hair when she saw Sabrina, then pawed the path with her foot.

Uh-oh. We've got a horse walking a professor. Looks like my allergy's still there big time.

"Hi, Morgan," Sabrina said.

"My name isn't Morgan. It's Greased Lightning Bolt," Morgan said firmly.

"All right, Grease. What are you doing with Baskers? He's supposed to be staying in my room." Sabrina had a mental image of Baskers escaping to his classroom and writing graduate-level biology info on the blackboard.

"I got a hankering to find a fox," Morgan explained. "I thought Baskers might lead me to one. After all, he is a hound."

Hound. Sabrina had heard that word so many times in the past couple of days, and not just because of Baskers.

Wait a minute! Baskers. Hound. Real name: Baskerville. Hound of the Baskervilles. Sherlock.

Sabrina snapped her fingers. "Of course, it's Baskers!" she cried, forgetting for a moment that Morgan was listening.

Morgan shied sideways. "What's with you?

You've got this weird look in your eyes. Scar-y!" she exclaimed with a little whinny.

"Calm down, Grease. I mean, whoa."

Sabrina's mind clicked away. *Deep down, I must feel guilty for conjuring Sherlock, because a mortal who overslept wouldn't have had the same advantage. Not exactly cheating, but almost. I guess seeing Baskers in Animal Communications class triggered my guilt allergy. And then I aced my English test, thanks to Sherlock. I've been a walking guilt machine, and I didn't even know it!*

Sabrina felt bad. How could she not have realized the reason for her guilt? But she'd been too preoccupied with all the switcheroos to realize how she'd actually been feeling.

Also, who turns down an A plus?

Sabrina studied Baskers, who gazed at her sadly, as if he'd given up all hope of ever being human again. "Baskers, you've been making me sneeze all along."

Morgan skittered backward, tugging Baskers on the choke collar.

"Be careful, Grease," Sabrina said, focusing again on Morgan and Baskers.

Morgan made a chomping motion with her mouth. "I've gotta go. I'm on the hunt for a fox."

Sabrina's head began to pound. Her guilt was

obviously still there, or Morgan wouldn't be acting like a horse. Hadn't Dr. Allerzapper said that as soon as she purged her guilt, all the switcheroos would instantly change back?

But clueing in to what's causing my guilt and purging it are two different things.

She felt incredibly frustrated. Learning what her diagnosis was had been hard enough, thanks to Bea's interference. Then, detecting the cause of her guilt had been even harder. Now, figuring out how to purge it looked like the hardest step of all. Meanwhile, the more she sneezed, the more she was advancing Beatrice's evil cause.

"I guess if I stay away from you, I won't endanger more mortals," Sabrina told Baskers. "But I've got to get you away from Morgan. Who knows where she'll take you?"

As Sabrina reached for Baskers's leash, she noticed the flute player dashing out of Huppman Hall.

"That chick with the long brown hair is really weird," he commented as he raced toward Sabrina. "I think she could really use some professional help."

You're not kidding. And so could Morgan. So could Baskers. And so could I!

"I almost forgot she was there, when she

suddenly hissed at me. That was a little too freaky for me. I took off with my flute and never looked back."

"Did she follow you?" Sabrina asked, scanning the front of the building for a sign of Roxie.

The guy pursed his lips. "I wouldn't know. I just ran."

He reminds me of a fish with his lips pursed like that, Sabrina thought.

Baskers shook his head, his ears flapping loudly, as he strained against the tight leash.

"At-choo," Sabrina sneezed before she knew it.

Morgan reared backward, tugging wildly on Baskers. "What's all that colored stuff coming out of your mouth?" she asked. "Fireworks? Get me out of here!"

The flute player grabbed Sabrina's arm with a grip so tight that she cried out. "Ouch! What are you doing? Let me go!"

But one look at his bright red face and popping eyes told her she had an emergency on her hands.

"What's wrong?" she asked. "Are you having an asthma attack or something?"

"The air is so stuffy," he gasped. "I can't breathe. Take me to a swimming pool before I die!"

Chapter 11

"Swimming pool? Oh no, you're a fish!" Sabrina cast her mind back to the thought she'd had while she sneezed.

Why wasn't I more careful with my thoughts?

But it had all happened so quickly—Baskers shaking himself and her sneezing and her brief thought about the fish. She'd barely registered what was going on until it was too late.

Too late? What if she couldn't get this fish into water on time? At least the other animal switches hadn't been dangerous, except maybe for Roxie's teeth.

On second thought, he's a fish with lungs. Why can't he use them to breathe? "You don't need a pool," she told him. "I'll teach you how to use your new lungs. Just chill out and take a moment to practice breathing with them.

Like this." She breathed deeply in and out.

The flute player did his best to mimick her, taking short, nervous breaths.

"Close," she said, encouraged.

"I feel a little better," the guy admitted, sounding as if he'd just run a marathon, "but I feel very uncomfortable out of water. It's just not *me*."

"I'll take you to the gym," Sabrina suggested. "You can hang out in the pool while you get a grip on being . . . human."

He squeezed her arm tighter.

"Don't worry," Sabrina said calmly.

Sabrina saw that in all the confusion, Morgan had sneaked away with Baskers.

"Come on," Sabrina said, and led the way down the path to the nearby gym with the flute player hanging on her arm. Once there, she dragged him up the front stairs and through its large metal doors.

"Hold on, we're almost there." Sabrina led him down the stairwell to the pool. "Are you ready?" she asked, and pushed him into the water, clothes and all.

Sabrina stepped back to avoid the splash. The flute player dove under water and resurfaced, sputtering. "This water is worse than the air," he complained, coughing. "What's in it?"

"Water, chlorine, a couple of other swimmers."

The two other girls in the pool looked at Sabrina with interest. "Is this some kind of fraternity stunt?" one of them asked Sabrina. "Why is he swimming in his clothes?"

"Uh, yeah . . . ," Sabrina said unconvincingly.

Meanwhile the flute player was happily swimming in the water, diving and jumping like a salmon. "I think I'm getting the hang of this," he called, taking deep breaths of air as he resurfaced. "Thanks so much for your help."

Sabrina left him spinning in the water, flapping his shoes like a fish tail as he frolicked in front of the puzzled girls.

How long is he planning to hang out there? I hope I can switch this spell before he turns from human fish to human prune.

Sabrina hurried outside. *Now what?*

"Hey!" a familiar voice called.

"Josh!" Sabrina said. He was walking toward her from a path that connected with a main sidewalk on the periphery of campus where some shops were located.

Sabrina's heart sank as she saw him holding a wire cage with five fat mice inside, one of which was busy on a treadmill.

Sabrina sighed. "What are you doing with those mice?" she asked suspiciously.

Josh licked his lips. "I bought them at the most awesome pet store. It specializes in small, juicy rodents—not only mice, but rats and gerbils, too. You ought to check it out sometime."

Sabrina grimaced. "No thanks. Did you buy them to be your . . . pets?"

"Not really. I bought them for soccer."

"Since when do mice play soccer?"

"They don't. They're the balls," Josh explained. "I know you probably think I have an unfair advantage over them. But that's okay. The game can be very challenging when they try to escape."

"I see," Sabrina said. "So what happens when you catch them?"

"I don't 'catch' them. I bat them into the goal. My dinner plate."

Dinner? Sabrina peered at his prey.

"Um, how's the newspaper these days, Josh?" Sabrina quickly tried to change the subject. "Remember? Your job?"

Josh frowned. "I've changed careers. I mouse-sit for a living." He lifted the cage and gloated. "But I gotta go. It's time for a match." Josh grinned and took off across campus before Sabrina could stop him.

This spell has gone way too far. Sabrina sat down on a nearby bench to think. She knew that summoning Sherlock was the reason for her guilt, but what could she do to get rid of it?

And the answer came to her. *The test.* Much as Sabrina hated to admit it, she knew she hadn't earned an A plus on her *Hound of the Baskervilles* quiz. She bit her lip. *Okay, I know what I have to do.*

A feeling of doom bubbled up inside Sabrina's chest as she faced up to a chilling prospect: spilling her guts to Dr. Kramer.

But I can't tell a mortal that I conjured Sherlock, so what do I say?

Sabrina checked her watch. Fifteen minutes until English. *Gotta move.*

Gathering her books, Sabrina headed over to class. With ten minutes to spare, she was relieved to find Dr. Kramer reading her notes in the empty classroom.

Seeing Dr. Kramer's gray head bent over her papers, Sabrina felt a final spurt of terror, like a sky diver before making the great leap.

Sabrina squared her shoulders. *This is it—my moment of reckoning.*

"Uh, Dr. Kramer?" Sabrina said hesitantly.

The professor looked up. "Yes?"

"I'd like to talk to you about something."

Dr. Kramer glowered at Sabrina from over the rim of her spectacles. "About what?"

Sabrina paused. "The test."

Dr. Kramer smiled gleefully. "I'm impressed by your fortune-telling skills, Sabrina. How did you guess we were having one today?"

"We are?" Sabrina said, and gulped. Her heart pounded away. "I meant the test we had yesterday on *The Hound of the Baskervilles.*"

"Aren't you pleased with your grade?"

"Of course I'm pleased with my grade. I mean, I am and I'm not."

"Continue, Sabrina," Dr. Kramer demanded. "We only have a few minutes before the other students arrive, and I want to give them the whole period for the quiz if they need it."

Students straggled in, setting down books and backpacks on desks around the room. Fortunately no one was close enough yet to hear Sabrina talk. Still, she lowered her voice.

"I have a confession to make, Dr. Kramer." Sabrina's voice gained urgency as she realized she had a limited time to talk. "My pop quiz grade was a fraud."

Dr. Kramer shot her a stare that could freeze an erupting volcano. "What?" she asked.

"See, I read most of *The Hound of the Baskervilles,* but I didn't have time to finish it. Instead, I . . . I . . . used a study aid!"

Dr. Kramer frowned. "What kind of study aid?"

"It was just, um, a shortened description of the book. But it had all of the essential elements."

"I guess so, because you certainly fooled me." She drummed her fingers on the desk while Sabrina held her breath, bracing herself for the ax to fall.

Is she going to flunk me? Expel me for cheating? Roast me on a grill?

"Well, Sabrina," Dr. Kramer continued after a long terrible pause, "I'm disappointed— especially because you used a mere summary to take the place of reading a classic. There's more to a book than the plot. The language, the style, the tone—the book is a sum of its many parts."

Sabrina's heart plunged. *Just get this over with. I can take it.*

"I am, however, impressed by your honesty." A tiny smile formed around the corners of the professor's lips. "You're very lucky Sabrina, I've already decided not to count that quiz toward anyone's final grade. I trust I can count on you to finish *The Hound of the Baskervilles,* correct?"

"Absolutely!" Sabrina promised.

"What's important is knowing and appreciating the book, not getting the best grade," Dr. Kramer said passionately. "That's a lesson so few college students follow these days. Students forget about the pleasure their studies can give them." Her face clouded over. "And they so often forget about honesty."

"Honesty is the best policy," Sabrina said brightly. *Except when it comes to admitting you're a witch.*

"Glad to hear it. In any case, Sabrina, even though I am no longer counting the grades from yesterday, you'll have an opportunity to redeem yourself."

"Really? How?" Sabrina was suddenly feeling very confident. Dr. Kramer was not only going to let her keep her self-esteem, but she was giving Sabrina a chance to make up for what she had done. "Thanks for another chance."

"Don't thank *me*, Sabrina. Thank the pop quiz I'm giving today on 'The Tell-Tale Heart.' I'm definitely counting this one toward the final grade."

Sabrina turned white. In all the switching mayhem, she'd only given 'The Tell-Tale Heart' a quick read. But at least she'd finished it.

Dr. Kramer went on. "Since Sir Arthur Conan Doyle and Edgar Allan Poe are both classic suspense writers, I'm assigning their work back-to-back. You didn't use a study aid on this story, did you?"

"Another study aid? No way. I've learned my lesson. I'll try my best on the test today. And I promise I'll finish *The Hound of the Baskervilles* tonight."

"Very good, Sabrina. I trust you on that. We've only got a couple more minutes till class. Why don't you take a seat."

Sabrina felt an enormous weight slide off her shoulders like a huge rock avalanche tumbling down a cliff.

It's as if Dr. Kramer gave me some sort of anti-guilt blessing. I feel ten tons lighter.

As Sabrina turned away from Dr. Kramer, she did a double take. The Greek king Sisyphus—condemned to Hades to push a rock uphill for eternity to atone for his earthly sins—was wearing a white shift, sandals, and laurel crown and was pushing a guilt-boulder away from Sabrina toward the classroom door.

Sabrina knew he was invisible to everyone else, but she couldn't help scooting over to him and murmuring, "Thanks, Sis. You've taken a load off my shoulders."

"No problem, Sabrina," he said cheerfully. "This is my new job. Gathering guilt-rocks and pushing them to the Ends of the Earth." He paused a moment to wipe the sweat from his brow. "You should see some of them. I mean, yours was nothing compared with Genghis Khan's."

"Genghis Khan? The medieval pillager who destroyed life wherever he found it? Was he even capable of guilt?" Sabrina asked.

"Big time," Sisyphus confided. "Too bad he lived before psychotherapy was in. His guilt-rock was murder on my back."

He continued pushing Sabrina's guilt-boulder down the hall, just as Miles hurried into the corridor.

"Sabrina, what are you doing out here talking to yourself?" he asked, scanning the area. "Do you see aliens?"

"Miles, you're not a bee!"

"Huh?"

Sabrina shook her head to clear it. "Sorry, Miles, I meant . . . I was talking about your grade. See, we're having another pop quiz in English—this one's on 'The Tell-Tale Heart.' So I meant here's your chance to get an A, not a B." *Miles is back to his old self. Which means all the other switcheroos must be okay too. Dr. Allerzapper was right: The moment I purged my guilt, all the switches switched back. Woo-hoo!*

Miles gulped. "Or a C," he told her anxiously. "It's so weird—I have no memory of the past day.

But I'm pretty sure I didn't spend it reading 'The Tell-Tale Heart.' "

"I'm kind of in the same boat," Sabrina admitted. "I mean, I read it, but not very carefully."

"I wish that I had some sort of summary or study aid to review. Oh well, too late now."

Study aid? Ouch!

Still, Sabrina couldn't help a momentary regret. Even though she knew she wasn't going to conjure Edgar Allen Poe for help, she thought he'd be fun to talk to since she really didn't get to spend any time with him when her aunts invited him for Halloween a couple of years ago.

But she quickly banished the thought. *I'll just have to face whatever Dr. Kramer throws at us. I'm sure I'll do fine without magic.*

Sabrina and Miles found two desks next to each other as Dr. Kramer passed out the test sheets. Once more, there were three essay questions. And once more, Sabrina finished early.

She handed in her answers to Dr. Kramer, crossing her fingers about the results.

Chapter 12

The bell to end class finally rang.

"For those of you who finished your tests early," Dr. Kramer announced, "you can pick them up here, corrected." She patted a small stack of graded papers on her desk.

Sabrina and Miles exchanged anxious looks. "Here goes nothing," Miles said, standing.

Sabrina followed him up the aisle. Dr. Kramer was sitting ramrod straight in her swivel chair, presiding over the class.

"Miles, you can do better," Dr. Kramer declared. "C." She thrust his paper at him.

"Could be worse," Miles said as he scanned Dr. Kramer's comments.

Dr. Kramer drew herself up as far as her diminutive height permitted. "That's ambition for you!" she exclaimed, her voice dripping with sarcasm. Turning to Sabrina, she said, "Here's your test back, Sabrina. Nice job—B plus. You didn't use as much detail as you did on the *Baskervilles* test, but you showed a good command of Poe's themes. I'm happy. Hope you are, too."

"Thanks, Dr. Kramer," Sabrina said. "What are you going to test us on tomorrow?"

"Tomorrow's Saturday," she replied. "But for Monday I want you to read *The Turn of the Screw,* by Henry James—another tale of suspense. And I'm not telling whether we're having a pop quiz. It wouldn't be 'pop' if I did."

After class Sabrina rushed home to Baskers, while Miles headed to his astronomy class. Sabrina wanted to make absolutely sure her guilt allergy was gone, and the quickest way to do that was to see if Baskers still made her sneeze. Also, she wanted to inspect him for any signs of Dr. Cartwright's spirit still lurking inside.

She held her breath, opening the door to her room. Baskers was curled up asleep at the foot of her bed, just where she'd left him.

"Baskers?" He lifted his head and stared at her curiously. "Let me give you a hug." She went over to him and buried her face in his furry neck. No sneeze. "Encouraging so far," she murmured, straightening, "but I still need to convince myself that you're not Dr. Cartwright."

She snapped her fingers and recited,

"Let me be clear
That this animal here
Is not man but beast.
Let him happily feast
On dog biscuits five.
Arrive!"

Five dog biscuits instantly appeared in Sabrina's hand.

"Here, Baskers, boy," she called, placing a biscuit on her outstretched palm. He sprang to attention, pricking up his ears while his sniffing went into overdrive.

Baskers opened his jaws and chomped, gobbling the biscuit with a blissful look. "Welcome back to your body, Baskers!" Sabrina exclaimed, giving him a major hug. She cocked her head, studying him. "Unless Dr. Cartwright nurtured a secret passion for dog biscuits."

Baskers licked her face, a long slurpy appreciative dog kiss. "No way would Dr. Cartwright do that—he's much too shy. Uh-oh, speaking of Dr.

Cartwright, I'd better go rescue him from my aunts." She grabbed the leash from the top of her bureau. "Baskers, let's go. It's time you and your master were reunited."

A few minutes later Sabrina and Baskers arrived at her aunts' house. "Is anyone home?" Sabrina called out from the empty front hall.

"Sabrina, I'm in the kitchen," Zelda replied, "with Mortimer."

Sabrina led Baskers into the kitchen, nervous about what she'd find. Even if Allerzapper was right about the people having no memory of the last two days' events, Dr. Cartwright would have found himself curled up on Sabrina's aunts' floor next to a chew toy. Sabrina hoped Aunt Zelda had given him a good explanation for *that*.

But no explanation was necessary. Sabrina found Dr. Cartwright happily sipping a cup of tea at the kitchen counter while Zelda served him.

"Hello, Sabrina," she said, barely glancing at her niece as she placed a sugar bowl and a small pitcher of milk in front of the professor. "Mortimer, would you like some freshly baked chocolate-chip cookies?"

"Thank you, Zelda," he replied, blushing as he took two cookies from the plateful she offered. He bit into one. "Mmmm. You've sure nailed the laws of physics when it comes to baking," he added.

"Something Einstein never learned," Zelda said, shaking her head. "His cookies were always dreadful."

"You knew him?" Dr. Cartwright asked.

"Oh—I knew people who knew him," Zelda said quickly.

"Sabrina!" Dr. Cartwright said, as if he'd only just noticed her. "What are you doing with Baskers?"

"Um, he must have escaped from your apartment," Sabrina fudged as she poured Baskers a bowl of water. "I found him wandering the campus."

Dr. Cartwright frowned. "Poor Baskers," he said to his dog, patting him affectionately. "Are you hungry?"

Sabrina shot a wry glance at Aunt Zelda. "I doubt it. He looks pretty happy."

"It's funny," Dr. Cartwright said, wrinkling his brow, "but I feel as if I've had amnesia or something. I can't remember a thing that happened to me since I brought Baskers to Animal Communications class yesterday. The next thing I knew, I was lying on a blanket in Zelda's kitchen a half hour ago."

Zelda looked peeved. "You don't remember the

oysters, steak, and lemon mousse that I served you last night for dinner, Mortimer?"

"Not specifically. But I have a wonderfully pleasant feeling about the past twenty-four hours, as if I just woke from a fantastic dream. And Zelda, for some reason I feel as if I know you so much better now! I'm glad you invited me to what sounds like was a sumptuous repast, or I wouldn't have had the courage to now ask you out on a date."

"Ooh, Mortimer, you're a hound dog!" Zelda teased.

Dr. Cartwright grinned. "I seem to be now, yes." He laughed, blushing again as he sipped his tea.

The front door opened, then clicked shut as footsteps sounded in the hall. "Zelda?" Hilda called out, bursting into the kitchen. "Is the dog still . . . ?"

The instant Hilda registered Dr. Cartwright politely drinking tea, her mouth snapped shut. "Oh, hello, um . . . have we met?"

Zelda introduced her sister to Dr. Cartwright. After a moment of chitchat, the professor checked his watch. "Excuse me, but I've got to go prepare my speech for the award dinner to-morrow night. And I also want to let the biology department know I'm well again."

After the professor left with Baskers, the three witches compared notes. Zelda confessed that she had let Dr. Cartwright out of his crate that afternoon to play fetch. But after fifteen minutes of chasing the Frisbee, he'd had enough and had come back inside to rest. "The next thing I knew," Zelda said, "Mortimer staggered to his feet and asked where he was. I had to think fast. I told him he'd been knocked out in class yesterday when a stray baseball flew through the window and hit him. Because he had no family close by, I offered to nurse him back to health."

"By throwing Frisbees for him?" Hilda asked.

"By cooking him meals," Zelda retorted. She turned to Sabrina. "You haven't told us, Sabrina—how did you manage to purge your guilt?"

Sabrina briefed her aunts on how she'd figured out what had caused her guilt and then how she had faced Dr. Kramer in order to send it packing.

"You were very brave, Sabrina," Zelda said approvingly. "And congratulations on your B plus."

Hilda said, "I figured that the spell had been broken when Josh changed his coffee shop order from a glass of milk to an espresso. So I rushed home to see if we still had a dog." She pointed at Dr. Cartwright's crate, and it disappeared in a puff of hair and smoke. "Whew! Was Dr. Cartwright shedding? I hope he still has some hair," she added with a little cough.

The toaster suddenly popped with a message from the Other Realm. Besides making toast, the magical kitchen appliance conveyed messages to the Spellmans from the Other Realm. Zelda pulled out the message and read it.

"'Sabrina Spellman and Salem Saberhagen are hereby summoned to a meeting of the Witches' Council as witnesses for the Realm against Beatrice Bodenheimer-Brown for her scheme to take over the world. Please make your appearances at six o'clock Friday evening.'"

Zelda shot a glance at her sister. "Let's go with them, Hilda. We can lend support to Sabrina and Salem if they need it."

"Me? Testify against Bea?" Salem hissed as the witches gathered with him around the linen closet.

"You and Sabrina overheard her scheme," Zelda answered. "This afternoon I sent a message to Drell letting him know how dangerous Bea still is. Obviously he took my warning seriously and decided to try her, and the council needs witnesses to support its case."

"Bear witness against my beloved?" Salem spat. "How can they make me do that? I'm racked with guilt."

"I hope you don't come down with a guilt allergy, too, Salem," Hilda said with a worried frown.

"Don't be so sentimental, Salem," Sabrina scolded. "You know you don't love Bea anymore. You're just trying to get us to feel sorry for you so we'll conjure you more sardines."

"The kid's good. I'll give her that," Salem murmured as they all stepped into the linen closet.

Moments later the Witches' Council convened. Salem and Sabrina waited at the front bench to be called to the witness stand while Bea sat in shackles at a side bench. Drell, the enormous dark-haired head of the council, arrived in his flowing wizard's robes and called the trial to order. Bea, unlocked from her shackles, was summoned to the witness stand.

After waddling up to the stand on her stumpy legs, Bea—too stout to jump—had to be lifted by a guard onto the chair.

"Is it true that you, Beatrice Bodenheimer-

Brown, continued your wicked plot to take over the world in spite of your nonmagical bulldog form?" Drell asked sternly as Bea slumped, sullen and drooling, in the witness stand.

"I plead the Fifth!" Bea snarled, refusing to say anything that would incriminate herself.

"I call Sabrina Spellman to the witness stand," Drell said.

Sabrina and Bea traded places. "Tell us what you witnessed this morning, Sabrina, outside Dr. Finius Allerzapper's office," Drell asked her.

Sabrina told the courtroom about overhearing Bea talking to herself about her world-takeover plan. After Sabrina had finished, Bea's court-appointed lawyer, a snide, brusque young man with prematurely gray hair, cross-examined her. But he was no match for Sabrina.

"You say my client was inside Dr. Allerzapper's office while you listened outside. How can you be sure that what you heard was correct?" he asked her.

"Because the window was open and her desk was right next to it," Sabrina declared. "I heard her loud and clear."

Drell dismissed Sabrina and called Salem, who dragged his paws all the way to the witness stand.

"I'm not exactly impartial," Salem admitted, "since I once worshiped the ground the defendant walked on. But since I've been called as a witness for the Realm, I have no choice but to tell you this." He lowered his voice, as if speaking confidentially. "Beatrice confided to me that she was using Sabrina's guilt allergy to take over the world."

"Really? And how would this scheme have worked?" Drell asked him.

"What say we work out a little deal here?" Salem suggested, taking note of Bea's furious scowl. "I'll tell you what I know, and you get me out of the cat suit."

"You'll tell me what you know, and I won't add any more years to your sentence," Drell blasted.

"Well, since you put it that way, I'm happy to spill my guts. Bea hoped Sabrina's allergy would switch enough animals and people so she could boss everyone around. The animals would have powerful human bodies and obedient animal souls loyal to Bea. Simple, yet brilliant, really." Salem knew immediately that last remark was a mistake. "And very, very wrong," he quickly added.

After Drell announced that he had no further

questions, Bea's lawyer stood up for cross-examination.

"Did you ever discuss being paid in sardines to lie about my client?" he asked Salem.

"It was never put on the table. Neither were any sardines."

"You mean, you potentially would have lied if promised fish? I question the credibility of this witness, Your Honor, and suggest that we throw out his testimony. I rest my case."

After Salem had slunk down from the stand, avoiding Bea's ice-cold gaze, Drell reviewed his notes and consulted with a group of six council witches sitting in a semicircle behind him. It took them only a minute to reach their verdict.

"Will the defendant please stand?" Drell demanded.

Huffing and panting, Bea struggled to her feet.

"Ladies and gentlemen, our verdict," Drell announced, staring imperiously at the audience from his podium on high. "We find Beatrice Bodenheimer-Brown guilty of continuing her plot to take over the world. I hereby sentence her to live out her bulldog life in the Mortal Realm as a pet."

"Oh, please reconsider!" Salem burst out. "Turning a beautiful witch into a bulldog is bad enough, but to break her proud spirit by making her fetch someone's slippers? What is the world coming to?"

"Silence!" Drell cried, angrily waving his wand at the cowering Salem. "I'll hold you in contempt of court for speaking out of turn. My sentence stands. The Witches' Council has spoken."

"I wonder who will be her lucky owners." Sabrina whispered to Salem.

"Maybe us," Salem said hopefully.

"Salem, don't scare me."

Then Salem locked eyes with Bea, who fixed him with a glare so full of spite that he flinched. "On second thought, I hope not us. After my incriminating testimony, I'll be looking into the familiar relocation program."

"I guess she wasn't moved by your passionate plea for mercy," Sabrina remarked.

"She always was a toughie," Salem said admiringly.

The Faculty Club at Adams glowed with soft candlelight on Saturday evening as the city's science luminaries gathered to honor Dr. Mortimer Cartwright. Josh, who was there on assignment from his newspaper, had wangled an invitation for Sabrina as his so-called assistant.

Zelda was also there doing double duty as eminent physics professor and envied date of the guest of honor.

The large dining hall smelled of lilies from table bouquets as Sabrina and Josh entered the room. "Man, a black-tie event," Josh said. "I don't go to many of these. By the way, you look great tonight, Sabrina."

Sabrina glanced down at her long turquoise silk dress embroidered with silvery sequins. "Thanks, Josh."

Josh slipped away for a moment to take some pictures of Dr. Cartwright sipping champagne with his colleagues. Zelda, dressed in a long, strapless peach-colored satin gown with a daringly low-cut bodice, walked up to Sabrina. "How do you like my dress, Sabrina? Mortimer can't seem to take his eyes off it."

"Hope it holds up," Sabrina replied.

"Oh, I put a spell on it to make sure of *that*," Zelda said, glancing down at the snug front of her dress with satisfaction. "I couldn't find a thing to wear in the Mortal Realm, and the outfits I've been pointing up lately haven't had much zing. So I went to this Other Realm Web site, WishUponanOutfit.spell. You write on the site what you want, click the mouse, and then your dream outfit magically appears."

The two witches paused as Josh crouched in a nearby corner to get a shot of Dr. Cartwright high-fiving a friend.

Lowering her voice, Zelda said, "Sabrina, Josh seems back to normal, but tell me how your housemates are. Is there any hint of animal still in them?"

"All normal, or what passes for it with those guys," Sabrina told her. "Though Morgan was a little freaked to find herself in the starting gate at the track."

The orchestra struck up a lively jazz tune. "Hey, Sabrina, Zelda," Josh said, ambling over to them. "I have a free moment while Dr. Cartwright gabs with some Nobel laureates. Sabrina, would you like to dance?"

"Love to, Josh," Sabrina said, and grinned.

With Zelda guarding his camera, Josh and Sabrina weaved their way onto the dance floor. "I got some great candid shots of Dr. Cartwright," he told her, taking her hand. "But right after he gets his award I have to leave, to make my deadline. They're giving this story space on the front page."

"Congratulations, Josh. That's great!" Sabrina said.

"By the way, Sabrina," Josh said, "Life must really be agreeing with you. You've got this cool look about you tonight. Kind of like you don't have a worry in the world."

Sabrina flashed him a smile as she twirled under his arm. *That's because I'm guilt-free.*

About the Author

Mercer Warriner lives in Brooklyn, New York, with her husband, two sons, a cat, and a dog. She loves watching *Sabrina, the Teenage Witch* with her family and wouldn't mind if she had magical powers of her own. Mercer is also the author of many other books for children.